AF431303

MASTER CRAFTER

BOOK ONE: BETA 1.0 TEST

BY HARLEY VEX

CHAPTER ONE

"Okay, Mike. Reach that flag, and you're off to the races." Feedback fills my VR helmet as I turn my gaze upward at the black and gray castle that just might change my life.

My heart hammers. My palms sweat. I almost forget that I'm standing in my tiny apartment rather than at the drawbridge of Vox's build in Creationist, the Monster Crag Castle. The dark structure and mountain it's in are made of blocks, sure, but that doesn't take away from my nerves. Shadow-filled windows promise monsters and traps that even the most seasoned players will take at least an hour to conquer.

Typical. Vox, a famous gamer, is known for his challenging maps made in Creationist's blocky, yet amazing sandbox universe. He changes the inside of the Monster Crag Castle every week, adding new traps and secret rooms, and after months of waiting, it's my time to capture the obnoxious yellow flag on the highest tower. It's so far up that the flat cloud deck partially obscures it. The hazy, pixelated sun is setting behind me. Other players' avatars spawn in while I wait with a mix of Lego-like people.

Lexi221 has joined the game.

Bartman_SK has joined the game.

Half of the contestants this week have the default monk skin. Faces with plain smiles and pixel eyes. Brown tunics and trousers. Plain hoods the color of dirt. Hopefully, they're just noobs. Well, one guy at the end has downloaded a pixelated skin of The Rock. The pixels make what's supposed to be an intimidating snarl look like he's trying to take a dump. Yeah, scary.

I hold up my avatar's hand and flex my blocky fingers. At least my skin is just a guy with jeans, a black T-shirt, and glasses that my sister Natalie made for me. I'm trying, but not too hard.

Until now.

I've been waiting months for this.

Natalie's relying on me.

If she loses her job and can't pay her medical bills—

,_andCupid has joined the game.

I blink, taking my attention off the feed at the bottom of my view. "The flag," I say out loud, refocusing on the Monster Crag Castle. I won't get paying live stream subscribers for nothing. I've got to entertain. Prove my skills. And get that sweet flood of new subs every winner of this weekly game gets.

My ten-year knowledge of Creationist is about to pay off.

Thousands of Vox's subs are watching, and some of them will follow me if I win. Though Vox's subs can't hear me, my few dozen trial subs, the ones watching from my first-person view, can. "Okay, guys. We're getting this flag. I'm going to make out with it. I've been studying this gorgeous castle for a year." I lift my hand and sink to my knee, pretending to admire the ugly, misshapen structure. I'm the only one. Vox is known for sadism, trolling, and most of all, killing.

And I, Mike Wattles, AKA *The Wattleman*, am all about exploiting Creationist to the hilt. When I break out on GameTube, everyone will see my mob traps and auto farms.

Ding.

Ding.

My heart leaps. Two new subscriber signups. Paid, too. Trial subscribers make a wimpy *tink* noise when they log on.

My first two paid subscribers.

My spine tingles. Just playing this map after climbing the six month wait list is paying off. I'm tempted to swipe my subscriber chat into my view with my glove, but I hold back. I need full focus.

"Whoever just subscribed to *The Wattleman*, thank you," I say, turning my head. "That means a lot to me right now. I'd chat, but I need to make sure I don't embarrass myself in front of you."

All twelve of this week's contestants stand at the mouth of the drawbridge which stretches over a river of pixilated acid. Straight ahead is an open doorway built to look like it's got fangs. The orange glow of sunset falls on everything. Soon the countdown will begin.

I need to vocalize my thoughts. "Okay, so I don't spot that off-yellow color that signifies a Falling Stalactite in those fangs. Those creamed a couple of players last week. And I don't see any signs of a Tripwire across the entrance." A few bats, harmless mobs, fly out into the deepening dusk. Bats avoid the nearly invisible Tripwires, providing one of the few ways for Players spot them from far off.

A floating green 10 appears before us on the drawbridge, and everyone stops fidgeting.

"And here we go," I say. The 10 turns into a 9 as darkness rolls over the sky, deepening with each wave. A single lantern comes to life far above, illuminating the yellow victory flag.

The monk beside me kneels as if this will be a footrace. Yes. A noob. I'll let him go first. No doubt he'll sprint across the drawbridge and into a trap right inside that dark interior of—

The drawbridge.

"Wait." I focus on the bridge. "Do you see what see?" I force myself to sing the line to that Christmas song.

Trapdoors look almost identical to Hardwood Planks except for the backward wood grains. And the drawbridge, today, is littered with them. In the dim light, even I almost missed it. They're triggered by Tripwires, but the Tripwires can be placed under the Trapdoors as well as above. They just work a bit differently that way, activating just the stepped-on Trapdoor instead of all the Trapdoors in the area.

"Well, we're in for a nice surprise," I say, knowing the other players can't hear me.

An orange 3 morphs into a red 2 which in turn transforms into a black 1.

And then with a loud wolf howl, Capture The Flag begins.

I hang back, watching the other avatars bolt across the drawbridge.

Click. Click. Click. Trapdoors trigger, opening one by one. The bottom of my view explodes with red death messages as other players land in the acid below, vanishing into puffs of smoke as they die. My mind races. There's a ten-second delay on respawning. I can see which trapdoors are open. They have a ten-second delay before closing, too.

"Time to go! And I hate parkour." I break into a run and jump onto the first solid piece of wood.

Acid spreads out below. The Rock is trapped on the low shore of the moat. He stares up at me, jumping up and down. "Well, someone's constipated."

I make my second jump, and then my third, heart racing. I'm almost at the entrance when the whooshing of players respawning sounds behind me at the start of the bridge. The Trapdoors close with a round of clicks. All sense of victory flees. I'm first. A target. Now to find a way to defend myself or set a trap before players or mobs catch up to me.

My vision adjusts automatically to the dark as I enter the castle. Three dark brick hallways branch off. All should have secret rooms. Time to choose. "The middle. Vox set up crushing walls there last week, so he likely won't this week."

I enter the arched corridor. Passing Lanterns, Potted Plants, and empty Barrels, I search the black and gray bricks of the wall for uneven surfaces. Nothing. No secret doors. And the hallway dead ends without a Loot Crate to speak for it. There's a hard-to-see hole in the ceiling, at the very end of the hall, but no ladder leads up to it. I wait for monsters to drop from it. Nada on that, too. "What? This can't be right." No hallway in Monster Crag Castle has nothing.

My heart races. I'm losing time. There's nothing here but a few Potted Plants, Barrels, and blocks of Straw. "Well, time to dumpster dive," I say, using the popular term for searching Barrels. Sometimes Barrels hold crappy loot. They can't hold anything halfway decent unless you hack the game. "If I'm lucky, I'll find an old Wooden Dagger." Cursing my luck, I lift the lid to the closest Barrel, eyeing the corridor for player names, which show through walls.

Three players have made it in. They're heading left. A few more death messages crop up. *MandyPie dissolved in acid.*

I reach into the Barrel. Its small inventory pops up as a gray box with square slots. Straightening, I tap each item and watch them zip downward into my inventory. Dirt Clod. Dirt Clod. Grape Seeds. Grass Clod. Single Unlit Torch. Stinky Fertilizer.

My pulse roars in my ears. "I'm feeling really good about my chances!" This whole corridor is a troll.

Two more players enter the castle, pause, and head right. No one ever has weapons at the entrance or I'd be dead. But elsewhere—

Bartman_SK has been killed by Cyndie_Kitty.

"Yeah. Time to figure something out." That's what I do best. There must be something I can use to my advantage. I eye the ceiling hole and then the Potted Plant. Then I think of the crappy loot I just found.

"Lightbulb!" I could make what players call a "ghetto elevator" by placing two Tripwire Bases beside each other and then an empty Pot on top of them. The Bases glitch and send the Pot skyward if an object or a player is placed inside. And if you want a controlled ascent, Grape Vines can act as guides.

But I don't have Tripwire Bases.

Or do I?

"I've got an idea! Ghetto elevator, here we come. And Vox, you are a sneaky rat," I say, running back to the entrance.

I've got Dirt Clods. They're a means to get under the drawbridge. Thankfully, no one is crossing it, though The

Rock is still stuck on the shore of the acid river. Vox would have placed the Tripwire Bases under the drawbridge, attached to either side of the bridge to hide them from view. I run to the side, careful not to fall over the rocky edge, and just barely see the bottom of a gray Tripwire Base under the bridge.

"Okay. This next part is easy." I crouch, sneaking to the very edge of the drop-off, and highlight a section of Stone below me. Then I place a Dirt Clod on it, which sticks since blocks in Creationist mostly don't obey gravity. That allows me to drop about a meter so I'm facing not one, but three square Tripwire Bases. Vox has three on each side of the drawbridge, anchoring the hidden Tripwires.

"Yes. I just need two." They're breakable by hand, so I punch the first, which pops off the stone wall and into my inventory. The entire Tripwire pops out of existence with it. Then I place another Dirt Clod beside the first, walk over the second Base, and do the same. "And ladies and gentlemen, I've got what I need!"

LilyHilly has fallen to their death.

I gulp. That could be me if this doesn't work exactly right.

I rush back into Monster Crag Castle and back down my middle corridor. The bottom of my vision is constant death messages. Someone respawns with a *whoosh* behind me.

I've got time and frustration on my side, so I ignore the others. The previous completion record was twenty-eight minutes. "We're about to make some magic happen. Ever seen one of these?"

I kick a Potted Plant first since I need it empty. I make a comment about plant cruelty as I work, and the Plant (yes, such a creative name) explodes into Sticks and Leaves. The items zip into my inventory but I ignore them, punching the Dirt Clod inside the Pot to break that, too. Bingo. Empty Pot. Now I need a second Pot to grow my Grape Vines.

I leave the Pot there for now and kick the other Plant. It breaks, and I remove the Dirt Clod. Then I tap my left arm to bring up my inventory. The bronze box appears in the center of my vision, with rows of smaller boxes inside that hold my items. I tap the Stinky Fertilizer, highlighting it. "I can't believe I'm going to have to thank literal crap for this." Then I tap the Grape Seeds and hit my left arm again, closing out my inventory. Now I'm holding one object in each hand.

I push one Pot under the hole in the ceiling, place the Stinky Fertilizer inside it, and then place the Grape Seeds on top of that. I stand back as Grape Vines grow, crawling up the wall and forming my guide. Vines can be used as ladders, but randomly break when you do, so you're lucky if you don't fall to your death using them that way.

"Wow. This is climbing up several floors," I say, watching as the green glow of the Fertilizer continues and continues. Finally, the Grape Vines quit growing up into the darkness and the Fertilizer reverts to a Dirt Clod.

There's no more room for them to grow. "And now, ladies and gentlemen, for the Mike Wattles Elevator Ride Into Probable Death!"

Step Two. I place the Tripwire Bases side by side, one on each side of the filled Pot. A faint Tripwire appears between them, cutting through the transparent Grape Vines, and I break the other Pot with my hand until it drops as an item and shoots into my inventory. I repeat the process to place it in my hand, where it appears as a shrunken version of itself, and I highlight the Tripwire (a move that requires finesse) and place the empty Pot.

It waits, ready for me to get in. Tripwires react to weight, but Salvos Corporation never fixed a glitch where such a short Tripwire doesn't detect weight until an actual player touches it. I jump, aiming for the Pot, and I find myself sitting inside it and bracing.

I fly upward with a *boing* sound and into the dark. Vines rustle as the Pot flies up them, but they don't break. They never do for objects. I sail up...up...waiting to take damage from some unseen trap. In the dark, I can barely make out the surrounding bricks zipping past. I spot a couple of ledges that lead to what must be secret doors, but nothing else.

I must be bypassing several floors of fun and adventure.

Excitement fills my chest. "Thank you, crap!" A faint, square outline of light draws closer. A Trapdoor that leads somewhere. My Pot stops at it as my head makes contact.

That's another glitch. Pots can be forced to climb Grapevines, but they're hard to get back down.

A double chime sounds.

A donation.

A freaking *donation.* My first one. And with the way I'm going, the start of many more.

I mutter a thanks. Thinking of Natalie propels me upward. Then I push open the Trapdoor above me.

"Oh, no. Here's the Probable Death."

CHAPTER TWO

This high floor of Monster Crag Castle is a deathtrap all by itself. Vox has no need to add crushing walls or falling acid to this space, because it's decorated with a black, vaulted ceiling, Lanterns, red carpet, and two rows of upright Coffins that stand between me and a stairway that must lead outside to the roof. A large window looks out on the roof just behind the Coffins opposite me, but without a means to break the glass, it might as well be a stone wall.

And Coffins can contain Vampires, who emerge when a player passes their location. No Tripwires needed. They're some of the toughest mobs in Creationist. With no weapons, I've got no chance. They'll kill me in seconds and even running to the stairs, gauntlet style, will have the same result. Vampires are also fast, can turn into Bats, and reappear in front of you in no time.

And if I die, I'll have no easy way back up here. The empty Pot will remain at the top of the secret shaft, unreachable.

"A Loot Crate," I say, eyeing the wall beside me. "Please, let there be a Hardwood Stake in there. At least then I can lure the Vampires out one at a time and maybe kill them." It's one of the few weapons that work, and if I could find a Vendor Block and enough materials to make a Switch, I could make a "stake shooter" and eliminate my need to get close to the vamps. But first, the crate. I remain half out of the hole, taking a breath. Moving too fast will get me killed, and the crate is just too far away to reach.

I stay in place. All the players are below me now, their names darting around the corridors. Another death message appears. "Okay. No rush. But I think I can just reach that crate." I lean towards the Loot Crate, which glows slightly. "Yes!" I reach out with my hand, and though I don't actually touch it, its big inventory opens for me.

"Oh. Of course," I say, eyeing the Weak Bow and the Arrows it contains. Useful against all *but* Vampires. But I tap them and they shoot into my inventory.

And then I see it.

The *steak.*

As in, the meat, not the actual weapon.

"Vox!" I shout, dragging out his name as my pulse races in my ears. I'd laugh if my whole future wasn't riding on this.

Then I take a breath. "Figure this out, Mike. You can do it." I talk as I think, discussing my plan. Hardwood Stakes are craftable—you fill all the slots of a Crafting Center with Hardwood Logs—but there's no wood here other than the Coffins themselves, and those drop Planks when broken. Some parts of the castle have Logs for rafters and support beams. And there must be Vendor Blocks somewhere to shoot toxic Potions and arrows at players. That'll work. I think of the ledges I passed on the way up and know I'll have to brave climbing back down the vines, and then possibly back up again.

Standing up, I break the empty Pot, putting it back in my inventory. Then I lower myself by crouching, and find myself holding onto the Grape Vines. I look down and move my hands vertically which sends me creeping downward.

"I am praying to the Creationist gods right now," I mutter, "and that's not a pun." The Vines creak as I creep downward, letting me know I could plunge to my death any second. But a ledge comes into view and I lean in that direction, and find myself standing on it. It goes in a few blocks before ending at an apparent dead end. "Success. We've found a new secret tunnel! Let's see if this is a sliding door or something simpler."

I hold my hand out and highlight not a block, but a panel with a frame. The back of a Picture Frame. They're often used to cover secret openings and Players can run through them, but most new players don't know this. But I don't barge through. On the other side is a player name—*MossHead13*—who is slowly inching closer.

"Shh," I hiss, though there's no need. I speak like I'm in a nature documentary. "Chances are, that player is armed."

The sliding sound of a Crushing Wall follows and MossHead13's name tag jumps backward.

An idea comes. "The *MossHead13* is navigating a dangerous environment. Crushing walls lie in wait for their prey, but the *MossHead13* is determined to get through and heed the call of the yellow Victory Flag."

I open my inventory and arm myself with the Weak Bow. Several arrows are needed to kill a Player, even unarmored, but only one can trigger a Tripwire or Trap Plate. And to activate either, a single arrow will work. I switch my tone back to normal. "Okay, I'm ready for this. We're taking that player's drops. Maybe he'll have something useful."

I step through the Painting and emerge in a long, gray corridor with alcoves and lanterns. I stand near spiral steps that must lead up into the Vampire room. *MossHead13* has the default monk skin and is holding a Staff in one hand and a yellow, glowing orb—a Sunlight Bomb—in the other.

"What the...heck?" I shout, stopping myself from cursing and earning a GameTube Adults Only tag. A Sunlight Bomb is a super-rare, OP item. I'm shocked. It's not something Vox would put in his maps. Making things easy isn't part of the program.

And a Sunlight Bomb would stun that entire room of Vampires for thirty seconds.

MossHead13 has stopped halfway down the corridor, watching as a Crushing Wall slowly retracts between two wooden support beams. He faces me. Raises his Staff. I aim my bow at him.

"No, I won't shoot him," I say, but the move has the desired effect. *MossHead13* leaps back, and just as he leaps over where the Tripwire must be across the floor, I switch my aim to that spot and shoot by pulling my right hand back and opening my palm.

The arrow flies and strikes.

And my timing is glorious.

The Crushing Walls close in from both sides with a deafening scrape and then a thud.

MossHead13 got squished.

"Yeee-esss!" I shout. The walls retract, and *MossHead13's* drops spin just over the floor. The Staff. The Sunlight Bomb. A bunch of Dark Bricks. No Healing Potions, though. "Let's grab that stuff and go stun us some Vampires." I leap over the Tripwire (thankfully, my Arrow is still lodged in the floor there, letting me know where it is) and tap the drops. They zip into my inventory.

After the Vampires is the roof.

And then, the final tower.

Then I leap back, put the Bow away, and equip the Sunlight Bomb. I bolt up the spiral steps. The chances of another trap being here are low. Stairwells just don't have much room to set up traps so Vox usually avoids them. And I'm not risking the Vines again.

The spiral steps lead straight into the end of the Vampire room. Coffins open with cheesy creaks as I bolt through to the next flight of stairs, raising the Sunlight Bomb. "Here we go!" I glimpse a couple of identical, blocky Vampires, both males with dark hair and black capes, stepping out of their Coffins, and I drop the Bomb to the floor. Both Vampires hiss as light fills the room, making me squint. They retract into their Coffins, which slam shut. "And behold, the roof!"

I reach the next stairwell, which leads to wooden doors that I push open. The slanted log roof of Monster Crag Castle greets me, and the final tower is on the opposite end. Rectangular clouds drift overhead, very close.

My heart soars and I want to sink to my knees and pump my fist. "There's the flag. I'm the first. I'm the first!" My spine tingles as I run along the roof and to the tower at the very end.

Until I see the Phantoms.

Whitish and glowing against the night sky, six of them fly listlessly around the tower while the yellow flag hangs still at the top of the spiral steps. I stop, my heart sinking back into my shoes. Phantoms have a fifty-fifty chance of possessing a Player when touching them. And then the Player loses all control of their movement.

And the tower is fifty blocks high, easily enough to cause death from fall damage.

"No. Oh, no," I mutter.

Phantoms can't be killed and will only ignore Players who are wearing Vampire Capes.

And I didn't kill any Vampires to collect their drops.

"Really? We have to go back and make a Stake Shooter after all?" I shout, careful to keep my language family-friendly. I search the roof, but it's all featureless Logs and wooden planks. Well, at least I can break the Logs and use them.

And I only need one Vampire Cape. The problem is, they're a rare drop. I'll probably have to kill multiple Vampires and not die in the process to get one. So yes, I'll need a Vendor Block and a bunch of Hardwood Stakes.

And that'll take time.

Already, the player names below me are so close they're readable. *MandyPie*. *Bartman*. Even *MossHead13* is just close enough to read, and he seems to be running up some steps. What gives? Why is everyone else having such an easy time? Usually no one's even on the third floor at this point in the game.

I only then realize that another Player has made it to the roof.

It's The Rock. With the username *Dynamite_Fart*. And he's armed with both a Hardwood Stake and a Spear. And he's also equipped a black Vampire Cape.

"Unbelievable."

He charges with the spear.

Even if he didn't want to kill me, I wouldn't stand a chance at reaching the flag first. There's no time to grab my weapons from my inventory. I can't run and do that at the same time. He strikes and my screen turns red as my shrinking health bar flashes to the top of my view. Then he stabs again and my health drops to a sliver.

And again.

Darkness fills my view. *You are defeated!*

A countdown timer ticks down underneath it, and when the ten turns to a zero, I respawn back at the broken drawbridge, standing alone, just in time to see the yellow flag far above drop out of sight.

CHAPTER THREE

Rage quitting Creationist while using a Virtual World headset can end badly if you throw the headset down after removing it. It's also tough stepping off the roller balls of the Virtual World platform.

Especially when you live in a cramped apartment.

But I rip the headset off anyway and return to reality. Stacks of pizza boxes. A couch covered in random junk. A TV stand of fast food wrappers and empty soda bottles. The plain white walls of the apartment seem to close in even though my roommates, Will and Steven, are gone for the night.

It's my world.

My only world.

And I'm stuck here for the time being.

Shaking, I set the Virtual World helmet down on the coffee table, balancing it on a stack of mail that includes my latest student loan bill, and then step out of the Virtual World Platform which is literally a giant cup of rolling spheres. It's three feet by three feet which prevents me from crashing into the TV or the table while I'm running through a game.

Or performing an epic screw-up.

"How did you let that happen?" I shout at myself, looking side to side as if the walls have answers. The noob...there's no way he should have...he broke the time record..."What *happened?*"

I want to throw my helmet at something. Anything.

But instead I stand there, stunned, staring at my helmet as the horn to end this week's game of Monster Crag Castle sounds. The lights of the inner display illuminate my bill. Then I yank off my haptic gloves.

No. I should have had that victory. All I needed to do was figure out one mob trap for that Vampire Cape. I would have grabbed the flag. Vox never leaves great equipment just lying out for players to grab, especially those who have no knowledge of Creationist's mechanics. Convenience is never part of his maps, no exceptions.

Something was different this week.

"My week!" I want to kick the Virtual World Platform.

I eye my gaming laptop on the kitchen table, which is live streaming a view of the castle's entrance to the dozen or so people who might still be watching. My helmet's still broadcasting to it through the wire running into the attached dining room. Anyone watching right now is being greeted by silence, and possibly my loud but distant ranting.

The noob. The Sunlight Bomb.

My week.

My phone buzzes with a new text. I ignore it and rush over to the computer. No sense in telling my few viewers what's happened. The silence speaks louder than words. Maybe once I cool down, I'll edit in some sad music for when I upload the stream to my *TheWattleman* channel later. A sense of humor might bring in a few subscribers.

I could have—

I hope *Dynamite_Fart* just got lucky and everyone realizes that.

I curse and slam my fist down on the table. At least I'm far from my helmet and that's unlikely to get picked up. And I don't care. One hundred to two hundred potential paying subs. Gone. That's three to five hundred extra dollars a month.

And with that extra money, I could have—

My phone buzzes again on the coffee table.

"Mike, why didn't you just stick to your play style instead of soldiering through with a Sunlight Bomb?" I ask myself. I'm not a warrior or a PVP type. For a moment, the Sunlight Bomb had given me confidence in an area where I lack talent. Maybe Vox added it as a trap, a new type of trap for people like me.

I let out a breath. Wait. My stunt with the ghetto elevator may have paid off. So may have my move with triggering the crushing walls. My gameplay wasn't a complete disaster. I lift my gaze from the dirty dining room table and face my laptop.

"Okay." I let out a breath. I turn off the live stream, then the recording, and save it. After the save bar fills and my computer's humming calms back down, I pull up my

GameTube dashboard. I scroll down past my recorded, but little-watched, uploads. *Mummy Grinder, Over 1,000 Items Per Hour! Automatic Electric Eel Farm Tutorial! Stone Golem Auto Breeder and Magica Gem Farm! Take Showers in Magica Gems!*

Then I reach the Community Activity section, heart thumping in my throat.

Your Notifications (5/16/2027)

CandiofSummer has subscribed to your channel!
AASalvosCorp has subscribed to your channel!
WillIAm has donated $1!
CandiofSummer has unsubscribed from your channel.
AASalvosCorp has unsubscribed from your channel.

My jaw drops.

A dollar.

And my two paying subscribers have just left.

My pulse roars in my ears. I slam the laptop lid shut. The computer hums for a bit before shutting down. I step back, taking a breath.

No comment.

I don't know how long I pace around my apartment, trying to calm down. I walk to my cramped bedroom. Sit on my air mattress. Get up and stand on the balcony, eyeing the overgrown grounds. Come back in. Pace some more. But at last, my phone's alarm goes off to signal that I've got to get ready for the Tenth Circle of Hell, otherwise known as my call center job at Everworld Hosting. I eye the digital clock on the wall. Eight. My shift starts at nine. It's been almost two hours since I exited Monster Crag Castle.

Happy Friday night.

I turn off the alarm after finding my phone near the pile of mail. Flopping down on the couch, I glimpse my messed-up, dark hair and a bit of acne under my eye that's persisted since I graduated high school seven years ago. Geek badge, and tonight I wasn't even a very good geek. I hide my reflection by swiping away the dark alarm screen and seeing a notification bubble from Natalie, my sister. A couple of texts. The ones I ignored and forgot until now.

I breathe out as my stomach turns.

Mike, good luck on Monster Crag Castle tonight. You'll get tons of new subs. Wish I could be there too.

Beside her text, her round photo smiles at me. People joke that we look like twins, despite her being two years younger than me.

Sweat forms between my fingers and makes clouds on the screen. I can't even respond. Not until tomorrow. What do I tell her? *Sis, I thought I'd be able to help cover all the testing. Take some stress off. But guess what? I can't. I hope your boss doesn't fire you.* How dare she get leukemia and have to take time off work to deal with making sure her numbers are still okay and she doesn't die.

I rise from the couch, needing to get out of there. Maybe I can ask my own boss for more hours. No, I should. That's what Dad would say, to go the extra mile for your employer and get rewarded. His words settle on my chest. Yeah, that's the way the world works, sure, but I'd been hoping for an alternative.

We're always short staffed at Everworld Hosting. This Creationist stuff just isn't getting anywhere. As I get up, my limbs feel as if they've turned to iron. Then I drag myself to my room and get changed into my black slacks, white shirt, and plain black tie. Tonight, I'd been hoping to stride into work, knowing I wouldn't have to ask for extra hours. That I could just keep working thirty hours per week and keep doing Creationist on the side.

With those thoughts heavy on my mind, I exit my apartment, walk down two flights of stairs, and emerge in the cooling late spring air of Charlotte. The towers of the city loom over me as I make my way past the carports and the parking lot of Cherry Ridge Apartments. I pick up my pace. Ah, the joy of being carless, but at least I can save a bit of money from not having those payments.

I walk past a black Mercedes with tinted windows, one that's parked near the exit of the complex. Weird. Why would some rich person live here? Maybe it's the owner who's getting rich off all the rent we poor people have to scrounge up and pay. My mood's already in the toilet, so I hunch up my shoulders and turn my back to the vehicle as I leave the complex and walk towards the city.

As I walk down the clearing sidewalk, watching the evening light morph from orange to purple, my head clears, piece by piece. I can always try Monster Crag Castle again if I re-enter the queue but it'll take months to get a chance to play. Vox only allows a dozen players a week to play the map to avoid spoilers and word getting out about new traps. And on GameTube which is saturated with Creationist content, it's hard to break out anymore even with my mob farms.

I'll need some other way to raise extra money for Natalie in the meantime.

And that's increasing my sentence at Everworld.

My sister is twenty-two, but she can barely keep up at her office job since her doctors want to subject her to test after test. She got diagnosed when she was eighteen, when blood work picked up something not quite right, but so far, Natalie has been lucky. Nothing's progressed so far, but after her doctor noticed something weird with her blood cells lately, she's been setting up more appointments for her to find out what's going on.

Her boss knows she has the chronic form of leukemia and might need sick leave at any point. The jerk nitpicks at her constantly for every tiny mistake, and I just know the guy is looking for a reason to fire her. I want to punch his smug self in the throat even if he does outweigh me by a hundred pounds. She can't afford to lose her insurance.

Work harder. Just do what they tell you. That's all you can do. Dad's sage advice. And for a little while, I thought we could escape.

I look at my hunched, skinny form in the glass window of a bakery. I'm almost running down the sidewalk, trying to escape my thoughts. What can I do? No one wants to hire a paralegal with less than five years' experience. My degree, meant to open doors, just slammed them shut. I should be buying my own house like Dad did when he was twenty-five. Maybe I'll have a shot at it in twenty years when my debt is gone and Natalie is healthy, but I'm not hopeful.

Natalie and I did everything right. And we're still failing.

I get so lost in my thoughts during my forty-five minute walk to the call center that by the time I notice the black Mercedes following me, I have no idea how long it's been there.

"What the heck?" I blurt.

As I turn the corner at a cell phone store, I spot the black sedan with the tinted windows lurking behind me like a monster. Its headlights are off which wouldn't be suspect if it wasn't just after sunset. That can't be the same car that was at Cherry Ridge Apartments.

But the tinted windows and the mean-looking headlights are the same.

I swallow. Sure, lots of people drive Mercedes with tinted windows, and they always hang around Cherry Ridge.

Yeah, right.

I up my pace. Coincidence, I decide. Maybe they're just parking in one of these parallel parking spots and the driver doesn't want to blind me. Hating that I look nervous, I use the store windows to gauge the situation. There's a parallel parking space open right next to me, which I rush past. Then I stuff my hands in my pockets and turn them out, making it look like I'm just looking for something.

Here I am, late for work. And I'm definitely not mugging material.

"That's stupid, Mike." Whoever drives this Mercedes is in no need to rob people.

I eye the glass of a vacant first floor.

Yep. The car's still following me, leaving the empty spot behind. And better yet, this side street is empty of everyone else. Any stores here are about to close.

My back prickles. Ahead, a few cars drive through an intersection. "Think, Mike. Don't screw up again tonight." I'm admitting to myself that this is creepy, and that ratchets up the fear from a three to a solid six.

The car, just ten feet behind me, rolls over a fast food bag that crinkles. It's keeping pace.

Plunging my hand into my slacks pocket, I wrap my fingers around my phone, hoping it's enough to convince the driver to move on. I pull the phone out, pretending to look at it. "You can go now."

The car speeds up just a hair, and my heart leaps until it slows back down, hanging at the rear of my vision.

The message is clear.

I'm hosed if I try to call the cops, and hosed if I don't.

Getting to a busier street is my best bet. The car keeps pace. I'm tempted to stop and ask them what they want. But my legs refuse to let me do that. They keep going. I keep going. I eye the crosswalk and the traffic light ahead. Grove Street. I'm close to work. But I'll have to cross right in front of this vehicle which I know might be the Bad Idea of the Year. I'm almost tempted to do that, just to prove that these jerks aren't freaking me out.

I reach the corner, turning to run across. Once that happens, I can make a mad dash to Everworld Hosting, dive in, and let an angel choir sing as I sink to my knees.

And the Mercedes rushes forward, stopping right over the crosswalk. *You shall not pass.*

"What gives?" My mind sharpens. The signal's red. If I head the other way, the Mercedes will have to wait to make a left. Sucks to be them. That'll give me time to come up with Plan B.

I turn and do a brisk walk towards the restaurant. Hey, I'm in work clothes. That might be good enough for them to let me in.

The traffic clears and the engine behind me purrs as the jerk makes an illegal turn.

"Seriously!"

Panic explodes and I break into a run past a closed bookstore, a closed music store, and a vacuum cleaner shop that's dim and empty inside.

It's official. They're after me.

The Mercedes pulls in front of me and parks beside the curb. I stop, seeing my chance to run back and force the vehicle to waste time making a U-turn. But the back door swings open, almost banging into me, and a large, burly man wearing a pure black helmet and an equally dark bodysuit bursts out. He looks like a cop from a nightmare future.

"What is going on?" I shout, hoping someone hears.

An arm wraps around my torso and I go down, landing on the sidewalk beside a squashed piece of black gum. The guy's weight collapses on me and then my arm's getting twisted behind my back. I should have called the cops. Trusted my instincts.

Now my day has managed to get a whole lot worse.

The dude yanks my other arm behind my back and before I can start yelling and cussing at the top of my lungs, a second guy appears in front of me. He's also in a black bodysuit and helmet. Featureless. And bigger than me.

He smashes a cloth against my face as the first, built like a linebacker, yanks my skinny self back to the car.

"Be quiet," the second dude says, holding up a finger. "Come with us or it's all over."

CHAPTER FOUR

Never let them take you to the second location.

I heard that once. Once that happens during a kidnapping, your chances of survival drop so much that you might as well plan out your will. I kick at the second dude, but he follows me closely, keeping the cloth smashed to my face so hard that I bring my teeth down on it.

I expect to pass out from fumes like in the movies, but I just keep biting down as the bigger guy yanks me backward into the car. I slide across leather seats and find myself squashed into the middle seat with two futuristic goons on either side. Awesome. There's a redhead woman in the driver's seat dressed in a regular business suit, and she doesn't speak.

"Umph!" I squirm a bit more, trying to climb over the second guy to get the door, but the locks all click.

"There's no point in fighting," the second guy, clearly the speaker of the two, says. "Enjoy the ride." His voice is low and muffled under the black visor of the helmet. I can see nothing beyond it. "And if you get out your phone, I'm afraid we'll have to confiscate it."

Then he removes the cloth, but I'm still sitting between the two guys. Man, I wish I worked out.

"Enjoy the ride?" I burst.

But the second guy laughs as if he's playing some college prank.

"Sorry. I don't see the humor in this," I say, hoping this is some bizarre prank my roommates are playing on me. Would Steve and Will do this to me? Why? We don't talk to each other much thanks to working different shifts, and I doubt their jobs checking out groceries and working gas pumps would pay for anything this elaborate. "You know, kidnapping is illegal." But I stay still, scanning the inside of the car. I've got to size up my situation, just like I do in Creationist.

Neither of the guys, nor the woman, say anything. She checks the street, a grin playing at her lips, before gently pulling away from the curb.

Prank, maybe. Killers don't smile like this and laugh unless they're total psychos, right?

I gulp, but let out a slow breath and look around. No one stops me. I spot no weapons on those suits the two guys are wearing. Both are one-piece bodysuits with blue stripes running up the sides of the legs, and have black, plastic plates on the chests, arms, and legs. Weird. And that blue scribble on the side of that guy's helmet almost looks like the fiery flag for Salvos Corporation. No, it's dark and I'm seeing things.

The doors are all locked and the tinted windows won't let anyone see me. And unless I can dial 911 with my phone in my pocket and without looking at it once, I'm not getting out. Every scenario involves me getting hurt or at the very least, getting knocked out.

I've got to get out.

My best bet is to stay conscious and talk.

"Are you debt collectors?" I blurt. *Way to go, Mike. Admit that you haven't been able to keep up on those student loan bills.* But if that's the case, then they won't kill me. Getting money out of a turnip is hard, but getting cash from a corpse is impossible.

The cute woman brakes behind a vehicle. Oh, *now* there are other people around. Then the truck moves and we roll down the street, farther from the call center, and closer to downtown.

"Mike Wattles," the woman says. She flashes a smile at me through the mirror as we roll through a green light.

Maybe I'm an idiot but her tone convinces me to unclench my fists and look less intimidating. The first dude lets go so that other than the fact that I'm still sitting between them, I'm free.

"You didn't answer my question," I say. "Who are you?" Maybe that's easier for them to understand.

The two guys say nothing. I sense they're letting the silence drag out.

"Am I going to survive tonight?" I ask.

"Depends," the woman says. She's still got that upbeat, but slightly evil tone. If my life weren't on the line, she'd be cute, but those green eyes make her look anything but.

"What do you mean, depends?" I lean forward in my seat, waiting for the guys to seize my arms, but they don't. I force down another breath of cool air. I've still got my phone. There's a chance they're joking. But the second guy is right. I've got no chance to call for help no matter what.

The woman doesn't miss a beat. "You'll see what we mean. Sit back and enjoy the drive."

"Seriously?"

The big guy taps my shoulder. I almost slug him but hold back because that would end in me flattened on the leather seat. Then I plunge my hand into my pocket. No one does anything. Maybe I can tap that part of my screen that says *emergency* and it'll call someone automatically. The cops can use GPS to find me. My kidnappers don't have to know until police lights are whirling behind us. I tap my phone, again and again, but if the woman is concerned, she's not showing it.

She turns left down another, narrow street. We pass an upscale apartment complex with tinted glass windows and then slow near an ominous garage door that's connected to the complex. As the Mercedes approaches, the garage door lifts, revealing orange sodium lights.

"Look, I'm not in any gangs and I'm not involved in anything you think I am." My mouth fires off as we turn into the garage. No, it's a tunnel that slopes downward and seems to lead into one.

"Are you sure about that?" The woman looks back at me as she eases the car into the tunnel. We roll downward.

So this is how it ends.

I grip the seat as the two guys beside me tense. We drive down...down...and then a heavy weight seems to crush my lungs. Natalie will never know what happened to me. Neither will my parents. And the worst part is, I don't even understand why.

At last, we circle around the ramp and pull into an underground garage that must be under the fancy apartment. A few other Mercedes are parked here. My survival instincts haven't died yet and I'm still breathing, so I scan the area. No one's waiting with baseball bats and guns. I doors that read *To Elevator* on the other side of the concrete room, but nothing else.

"Where am I?" I can try that. Stall them while I figure out how to run.

No one answers me. I can't take it anymore. "Where am I? You're making me late to work and I really have to get going."

The woman parks between two cars, as if she's trying to make sure there's a wall between me and sprinting to freedom, and speaks. "You're not going to need that job anymore, Mike Wattles." She turns the car off.

"So this is it," I say. "You're going to shoot me here. Look, I don't have a life insurance policy so unless you guys have taken one out on me—"

"This guy doesn't get it," the big dude says. It's the first time he's spoken.

"Well, Don, we don't exactly send out invites," the redhead says. "It doesn't work that way. It can't work that way."

"What is going on?" I ask, letting my voice rise.

"Well," the driver says, "Excuse our manners. If you get out of the car and behave, we'll show you. But unless you cooperate, I'm afraid we can't let you leave."

I'm at the second location.

Translation: I'm doomed.

The big guy, Don, opens the door and to my shock, stands there with the door open. He motions politely for me to get out. The other guy remains where he is, blocking my way back. I hesitate, but still no one gathers around the car to meet us. "I get to leave if I cooperate," I repeat. It's a question.

The woman steps out of the car, closing the door behind her.

"Don't tell me I have to push him," the second guy says.

"Unnecessary. We can stand here and wait," Don says with a shrug.

"Look, you tackled me before and now you're going to wait there like a bellhop?" I ask.

The woman laughs. "The correct term is 'valet.' And we have you where we want you now."

A bubble of anger rises in me. I've probably got five minutes before I'm due to start my shift and these people are making jokes. *I'm thinking about my shift right now?* Maybe they're even going to kill me. "One more time. Why am I here?"

The three look at each other as a long pause drags out. "Can't you see this?" Don points to the side of his helmet. He talks almost like he's sorry.

In the brighter light of the parking garage, I can see that the blue scribbles are, in fact, the Salvos Corporation logo. It's the flaming flag with fiery bars and a campfire in the upper left corner. Heck, it even says *Salvos Corporation* under the flag.

"Most people kind of get what's happening pretty quickly," the other guy says. "And they appreciate the little prank. But sorry, we don't film this. Candi will let you know a million times that we can't." He motions to the woman.

I sit there, stunned, and let my jaw slowly fall open. The woman—Candi—bites her lip. "Please don't tell me that you thought we were going to kill you."

This is a prank?

Or some other kind of setup?

Maybe I'm not about to die?

My mind tries to put together the pieces. "You followed me since I left my apartment, you know. And then Don here tackled me while you—"

"Matt," the second guy offers.

"—put a cloth to my face and shoved me into the back of a car with tinted windows. Then you told me I might not survive tonight and finally, you told me that I wouldn't need my job anymore." I want to believe that maybe I won some sort of Salvos Corporation top secret lottery and they're going to award me some new game system, but not quite everything lines up for that.

"Most gamers we pick up enjoy the thrill once they figure out Salvos is picking them up," Don says.

"Sort of," Matt says. "We're not quite Salvos." He goes to remove his helmet.

"Not yet," Candi orders, holding up a hand to him.

"Well, we scared the crap out of this guy," Matt protests.

"He hasn't signed any agreement yet," Candi says. "We have to be careful."

"Agreement?" I ask, scooting closer to the edge of the seat.

"Mike, a smart guy like you should be able to find the different meanings in what we said," Candi tells me, offering a wry smile. "You're so good at finding other angles to things that I thought you'd figure it out on your own. By the way, congratulations on your performance at Monster Crag Castle. We expected no less out of you."

Her words make me fly out of the back of the car. All of my fear vanishes and the world takes on a surreal orange light. I'm facing Candi, who is almost as tall as me. She's about my age with brilliant green eyes, perfect skin, and a great body that her suit hugs in all the right places. Then I shake my head.

CandiofSummer has subscribed to your channel!

"What do you mean? If you watched my live stream...you did watch my live stream. And then you unsubscribed."

"I needed to see your first person view and I couldn't have ads blocking the stream, so yes, I subscribed for a bit. So did Anthony Anton. I found your channel weeks ago, Mike, and I convinced the CEO to watch your performance tonight, too. Because of the way you played, we would like to extend an offer you can't refuse."

CHAPTER FIVE

"H...huh?" Anthony Anton, the head of Salvos Corporation, subscribed to me?

And what was that other username who subscribed and then left? *AASalvosCorp*. That checks out. Holy...if what she is telling me is true...holy...crap. "The CEO of Salvos watched me?" My voice rises in horror.

Candi just nods as I stand there on the concrete and close the Mercedes door. "I got the text that we could pick you up and extend our special offer."

"But I screwed up," I blurt.

"You did not," Candi says, turning away, inviting me to follow. Already, Don and Matt do so, leaving me standing there for a bit. Then she stops and looks back at me. "We planted that Sunlight Bomb, the Hardwood Stakes, and several other valuable weapons in the wrong hands so that Monster Crag Castle would favor those players taking the obvious routes to the tower this week. We could not have you reach the tower first, Mike, although you almost accomplished that. We were worried for a moment when you were about to make that impromptu Vampire grinder, because that would have led you to victory against all odds."

My ears ring. What am I even feeling right now?

"You set up my failure?" I follow, because I have no other choice at this point.

Offer. Salvos Corporation. How did they—

"It was necessary. You'll thank us later," Candi says quickly. She opens the door to the elevator, revealing a stairway and the red-painted doors to the elevator itself.

I squeeze into the small room. "Vox let you screw with his map?"

Candi busies herself pressing the elevator buttons. She presses the one labeled B, probably for basement. "Vox is working with Salvos Corporation right now. Something big is about to happen."

All thoughts of dying abandon me. I check my phone and no one stops me. I'm already ten minutes late for work. Whether I'll keep my job depends on my boss's presence.

But maybe Candi is right and I won't need it.

A tingle sweeps over me. What if this is my break?

"How did you find me?" I ask.

"Nothing online is truly private." She turns to face me directly as the elevator hums behind the doors. "Salvos has a database of all of Creationist's user accounts which include addresses and other billing information. It was no problem finding you. I think you'll be very useful. We need a player like you. And Mike, I can't believe your Mummy grinder didn't get many views. GameTube is not what it used to be."

I had spent much of that episode talking about how worried I was about Natalie's illness, so I figured I had driven people away with doom and gloom. But I can tell Candi's not lying.

"You didn't have to kidnap me if you just wanted to get some feedback about Vox's map. Ever heard of surveys?"

"No one takes surveys." She waves us into the elevator. Don and Matt get in first, and I can't resist.

"Okay. Fair enough," I say, getting in as well.

"I'm glad you're going to hear us out. You are in need, Mike."

"Are you going to offer me a job?" The words float out of my mouth as we stand, with my back to the elevator door. She's got me hooked. My theory about some kind of new gaming system makes sense because Matt and Don are decked out in gear I've never seen.

"Maybe, in a sense." Candi's tone drops a tiny bit. "More like an opportunity."

My heart thumps. Just an opportunity? That can mean a lot of things that don't include a paycheck. My unpaid internships were an *opportunity*. But I don't want to get on anyone's bad side quite yet even if Candi is cute. So I go to another question. "But why did you have to make me lose my tournament tonight?" If these people screwed me up on purpose, and they're just going to offer me an unpaid gig doing something, I'm going to be furious.

The elevator dings once, and the doors open, and I back out just enough to stop them from closing again.

Behind me, bright lights shine and I catch a hint of a blue glow, but before I get too far into this, I need answers. *The Wattleman* is not stupid.

"Why couldn't I be allowed to win Capture the Flag?" I keep my voice neutral, shocking myself.

Candi steps forward, ready to exit. "Because if you had won, you would have focused all your attention on Creationist.

"Well, not all of it. I would have kept my job because my sister is about to lose hers. Long story. I was planning to do both my job and streaming. I'm not crazy." As much as I'd love to give up that call center for gaming full time, I know it's not realistic. Dad's let me know a million times that the job has to come first, and my experience rolling a boulder uphill on GameTube crushed any dreams of him being wrong.

Candi nods, indicating she's heard it. Yes. The Mummy grinder video. I talked all about it. "Makes sense. But you had to lose tonight."

I place both my hands on the sides of the elevator, making sure no one can get out. Reality sucks. I can't be fooled. "Why, though?"

"Because Creationist is dying. People just don't know it yet," Candi says.

Don nods in agreement and Matt just stands there.

"It's the most popular game in the world," I say. "People can do anything there, build anything there."

"We had to detach you from Creationist, though. Soon, Salvos will stop supporting Creationist and stop releasing updates. That will happen in less than a year. You may have gained a couple hundred subs, Mike, but you would have soon lost them when the next big thing comes out on the market."

"Detach me?" My chest seems to hollow out at the news. Salvos stopping updates on Creationist seems like something that would never happen.

"Why don't you turn around?" Matt asks. "And you'll see why Creationist is about to dry up."

I take a breath. '

And then I turn around to face the basement.

Bright light and neutral gray walls greet me. Two rows of glass boxes, all six by eight feet, stand against the walls. I count four boxes on each wall, for a total of eight.

Wait. They're not boxes, but chambers.

Each box has a row of long blue lights on its ceiling and some familiar roller balls on the floor. Unlike my Virtual World Platform back home, the roller balls here are small, the size of marbles, and set on a flat surface. A glass door on the front of each chamber has the fiery Salvos flag on the front.

And players occupy two of the boxes.

Both wear the black bodysuits and the black helmets that Matt and Don are in. But while my kidnappers are lacking gloves, the players in the boxes are wearing black gloves made from some shiny material. One guy waves his hands in the air as if he's putting something together or moving parts into place. He splays his fingers out over and over as if shooting something from his hand. Another player, a woman judging from her height and shape, is holding an invisible object and swinging it at something I can't see. Then she runs in place as the roller balls spin and even rise a bit at times, keeping her from banging into the walls.

"So you really are Salvos Corporation," I say, frozen.

"Welcome to our testing room," Candi says. "Now, we all need to be able to exit the elevator."

I step into the room, finally letting everyone else out. "No way. This is too good to be true."

She grins. "For most, it is. Right now, this new game is in closed beta. Top secret. And Anton only wants fewer than ten beta testers right now. If you join us, we'll be up to a total of seven. We have plenty of builders and adventurers. But we need an inventor."

And then she winks.

"An inventor? What? So is this a completely new game?"

Candi reaches out and grabs the metal handle to one of the glass doors. "Completely new *experience*. Not only do we have a new sandbox game in the works, but we have a whole new virtual reality system that's about to take the world by storm."

Oh, no. She's got me. Tingling excitement explodes across my palms. Despite my kidnapping, I'm itching to step into one of those boxes and see what's engrossing those players. "So, a new game *and* a new VR system?"

The redhead knows I'm hooked. Her eyes flash and she flings a strand of her hair back, breaking her professionalism. "Precisely."

I can't hold back. "What's this game called?"

"If you agree to become a beta tester, you must sign a non-disclosure agreement. We've all signed it, so we can't give you any details. Conditions are so tight that we can't even give each other hints or talk that much about our experience."

"You're a beta tester, too?" I don't need to ask what a non-disclosure agreement is. I haven't found a job in my field yet, but I remember most of what I learned in my law books. Basically, you sign the agreement and shut up about whatever you're working on to everyone.

"Beta tester and recruiter," Candi says with a nod.

"Oh. Because it's top secret,'" I say, flexing my fingers to make quotation marks. "Tell me. Would I get paid for this and would that be in the contract, too? Everything needs to be in writing."

Candi puts up an instant mask. "The only detail I am allowed to offer right now is that you will receive free lodging in this building, Salvos's Charlotte office, in exchange for becoming a beta tester. It will be a requirement along with silence. Salvos is very serious about releasing no details of this game to the public until it is close to release and they've balanced the game."

"What else?" I think of Natalie. Beta testing a new adventure sounds fun and sends a thrill down my spine I haven't felt since first starting Creationist. "What about pay?"

"I cannot divulge that information. I'm sorry." She picks at the lapel on the front of her suit.

"You seem happy about this." Dread curls in my gut. I've got to be careful and scrutinize everything.

"To be fair, you also seemed happy to be walking to that call center. Did you know that Everworld Hosting is little more than a scam?"

Her words hurt and I flinch. "You know I work there?"

"Your place of employment is on your People Profile," she says, referring to my social media.

So she's been stalking me. "Well, you get right to the point," I say. "If you can't guarantee pay, I can't do this. I'm sorry."

Candi's face falls. Even Matt drops his shoulders. And I know the answer to the pay situation.

You have to do what you have to do, Dad would say.

I die a little more inside. To my shock, I'm not that angry. If they're right, me winning Monster Crag Castle wouldn't have done much, or just given me a little taste of a dream that would get yanked away from me again. "I'd love to hop in one of those boxes and play more video games but it hasn't gotten me anywhere so far. This is too much like an unpaid internship." I want Candi to refute me.

To open up and tell me that I'll get a paycheck. They need an inventor, as she put it. Maybe they can make it work.

But instead, Candi reaches into her front pocket and produces a black and blue business card. "I understand why you have doubts, Mike Wattles. Don't speak of this, but if you do, it's not as if anyone will believe you. Call me if you change your mind."

I swallow and take the card, anxious to see what all this is about but also anxious to leave. The agent's name is Candi Summers, spelled out beside Salvos Corporation's logo. She's listed as a Recruiter and her phone number and email shimmer when I turn the card. I tuck the card into my pocket, wondering if I'm making the dumbest mistake or the smartest move in my life. "Thanks," I say. "Can you show me out? I have to get to my job."

CHAPTER SIX

I did the right thing. Leaving my job for a stunt with no guarantee of pay is a stupid move. This call center might suck but it's a way to stay afloat until something better comes along, as Dad would say. They can always offer me some extra hours and I have benefits that I know about. With Natalie's boss getting on her case, I need those.

And I managed to sneak back into work two nights ago without the boss seeing. The assistant manager, Wendy, is pretty laid back and lets minor things slide.

Now I just have to work for my goal. And forget about the offer. It wouldn't have paid. The body language of all involved already warned me about that. And whatever game is in the works will come out soon enough. I'll get to see it.

What if?

"Shut up," I mutter, turning back to my workstation. The question keeps rising in my mind like some bad infection. Rubbing my temples, I adjust my headset. I'm once again losing focus on this call and the woman on the other end is almost in tears.

"...three hundred and fifty dollars. I don't even use the Plants For Profit website anymore. I stopped that business last year. I sent in an email request last month to take the site down and I still got charged." Her voice is one tone away from a croak. "Please, just listen."

"I'm listening, Ma'am," I say on autopilot. *The lines. Yes.* "I'll pass this along to our accounting team and see that they take care of it. That'll likely happen in three to four business days." I eye the Script Tips poster hanging on the wall on the other side of the room. *1.) Always say that you're listening. 2.) Buy time. 3.) When in doubt, "Pass It Along."*

Yet another piece of my brain turns into mush.

"Another tech told me this last week, after I got charged fifty dollars for some security package I never ordered!" She's losing it. "Croc Hosting used to be great. What happened?"

My gut turns. Around me, ten other call center techs handle calls from frustrated, unwitting customers. The heat in the small room rises off the computers towards the flickering florescent lights. A spark of life, sharp but alive, knifes its way into my chest. *Ma'am, they were secretly bought by Everworld Hosting last year, along with two dozen other good companies that now suck.*

"I'm hearing your concerns. I'm very sorry you're going through this." My own voice goes from a robotic drawl to something on the border of real empathy. Something in me is about to snap. Oh, no. I can't do this, but I sense there's no stopping the tsunami.

I eye my monitor's clock and the script on the screen. Six-thirty PM. I still have ten hours to go on my shift.

"The last guy told me this. I want your manager, for crying out loud! Someone who can do something."

The chair's making my butt go numb. Sweat gathers on my neck. I know what I'm supposed to say. *I'll leave a message. He'll call you back tomorrow.*

"Please. I can't afford this bill."

"Then tell your bank to block the charges," I say. "That's the only way to get them to stop. Call them right now and tell them to block every charge from Everworld Hosting. It'll show up as EHHosting.com on your bill."

The woman goes silent.

And at last, she speaks. "Thank you for the first decent advice I've gotten from you guys. You're a decent young man. Too many people out there are just in it for money."

A strange feeling fills my chest as she hangs up. It's warm, glowing, and has a slight magical tingle. I eye my screen for a few seconds. What have I done? *The right thing,* a little voice in my head says, before the sound of shuffling footsteps approaches my work station from behind.

"Mike Wattles. I see that, along with losing a customer, you punched in two hours late the other night."

The warm glow screams and pops out of existence.

I swallow.

And slowly, I rotate my chair around, despite my freshly ringing phone.

The air goes still thanks to the lumbering form of my boss, Landon, standing over me. Landon has his open laptop balanced between his forearm and his gut, with his tie pushed out of the way by the computer. He trains his eyes on his screen as if I'm a slug that he doesn't want to look at, but his eyes are narrower than usual. A bit of sweat gathers under his chin as he stands there, letting the silence draw out.

And I know that my fate is sealed.

What's wrong with me?

Why did I have to do something so stupid?

Are those nagging thoughts about the new game really getting to me that much?

"Hey, Landon. I'm sorry about that. I was getting harassed the other night by some jerks in a car and had to make a detour to get to work." There was that. Salvos Corporation made sure to make me late to my job which is another reason I didn't jump all over their offer.

"That is not a proper work ethic," Landon says. "Around here, we want workers who are enthusiastic about their jobs and who show up here on time. Our most valued employees work hard to retain our customer base and stick to the company line. In short, they are loyal to their employer."

I know what he's saying before he continues. We stare at each other, and once again he lets the quiet between us stretch into infinity. I hate that tactic. And at the same time, I don't understand the point. The sounds of other ringing phones and the conversations of other call center drones fade into the background.

But there's no going back now. That little spark of life rises in me again, and this time it reaches my voice box.

"I've been loyal for almost two years and haven't gotten a single raise. Or that Christmas bonus that got cancelled because the CEO was trying to pay off the stockholders."

I know I've struck a nerve. A flush spreads into Landon's cheeks and he tightens his grasp on his laptop. A tingle of satisfaction races up my spine even though I know what he's about to say.

"Mike. Get up. Get out. We'll mail you your check."

Close enough. I rise out of my chair, a volcano of fury blocking out my small victory. "Thanks, Landon. There's a very small chance you've just improved my life tenfold. Enjoy working for these scammers." And with that, I throw down my headset and walk out the door.

* * * * *

During the walk home, I manage to cool down a bit and breathe. What have I done? Dad's going to be furious. I'll have to tell Natalie. *That* will make her feel better about he boss setting her up.

"Great job, Mike!" I want to kick something but there's nothing on the street that qualifies.

I still hate Salvos Corporation for pulling a literal kidnapping on me the other night and putting me in this position, probably on purpose, but the longer I think about it, the more tempting Candi's business card looks each time I pull it from my shirt pocket. I've kept it with me over the past couple of days, wanting to throw it away and stop myself from falling for it. But I haven't been able to bring myself to do it, instead scanning every letter of Candi's email address and every character of her phone number.

It's a trap!

"Yes, I know it is," I say. Salvos might be a big company, but so is Everworld Hosting and they're nothing but a black hole. Then again, Salvos made Creationist. They gave something back to the world.

"Mike, knock it off." I half-jog past a coffee shop, drawing a stare from a guy inside who's reading a paper.

And then my phone rings rather than buzzes with a text. Great. That can't be good. Phone calls are reserved for just one of two things: scam calls and world-ending news.

It's Natalie. I swipe up to answer, knowing which possibility is the most likely one.

"Hey." I slow my walk.

"Mike. I thought you might be working but I wanted to try you anyway." Natalie's got a fake, high-pitched tone to her voice like she's nervous. I know her well, all the way down to her mannerisms.

"What's up, sis?" I swallow, knowing full well this won't be good. I stop and lean against a random building, trying to calm my nerves. I can't let Natalie get worried for me now. Bad news on my end might have to wait.

"I went to my follow-up appointment yesterday. And well, my white blood cell count was kind of high."

I pause as the whole world quiets. "That sucks. Do they think—"

"I should be fine so long as I keep this under control. The doctor said it wasn't that bad but I'll need to get some treatments. I guess it's a form of chemo and immunotherapy?"

"Sis, that sucks." My mind spins. I want to have some sage advice for her, so I work my brain for any legal stuff I might remember. "File for short-term disability *now.* Then you can't be fired because of any health related reasons."

"Trust me, Mike, I'm already working on it. The problem is—"

"Your boss has been building an unfair and BS case against you," I finish for her.

"And it has nothing to do with my health," Natalie says. "He's been trying to make me look incompetent for months. Last week, he wrote me up for not getting the sum on that spreadsheet right. I triple-checked it, so I don't understand how it was wrong when it got to him."

I swallow, knowing how meticulous my sister is with everything. Natalie's the accountant of a meatpacking company and was the top of her high school and college math classes. There's no way she's been making all these errors. Back in school, she was always the one leading class projects and pulling perfect grammar and grades. She hasn't had a "problem" since telling HR that she had a potential health issue last year. Hm.

"I'm sorry you're dealing with this."

"Don't be." She's struggling to stay upbeat because she has that breath at the end of her sentences. "I guess they say that young, fit people usually go into remission with this treatment so I'll probably be okay."

"You're worried." Natalie has a slower moving, chronic form of leukemia, but it's scary all the same. The doctors have been watching her for years. Thankfully she hasn't needed any actual treatment until now.

She's silent for seconds. "Mike, you know me too well."

"Well, we're almost considered twins. You might have to spend time out of work. The short-term disability will cover that part. It beats nothing. And once you're out of work, Pig Man can't find any way for you to have, quote on quote, screwed up."

"Mike, that makes sense. Thanks. I feel a bit better now. But I still want to keep working if I can."

I gulp because I don't. Pig Man has been sneaky and he won't stop now. I want to vomit or better yet, wrap my hands around her boss's throat. "You shouldn't have to go to work in that office when you're down from the treatment. I know chemo can be brutal."

"Well, I'm going to have to do my best. If I get canned, insurance is gone in thirty days. Not that it would make a ton of difference. It's crap insurance."

The entire sky, though now clear and full of stars, feels as if it's crushing down on me. I can barely breathe. "Hold on, Natalie. I...I asked for more hours at the call center and they gave them to me."

"Don't kill yourself. Mike, you're always doing too much. And you're better than that call center. I know Dad's always saying to wait for something better, but you know what? Maybe sometimes we have to go out and find it."

A strange feeling, like the universe is trying to tell me something, sweeps over me.

"I do this because you're my kid sis." I force a gleeful, evil tone into my voice even as I call myself a piece of crap for lying. "Just relax and get better, okay?"

We end the call there.

I'm halfway back to my apartment, but I don't put away my phone. Instead, I pull out Candi's business card again and begin to dial.

Maybe, just maybe, there's a way I can force this to work.

CHAPTER SEVEN

Maybe I'm a hopeful idiot, reverting back to when I started college, thinking my Paralegal program would open up a world where I could swim in piles of gold coins. But I know full well it'll take months to find a paralegal job if I'm lucky. All the jobs in my area want five years of experience. Applying just earns me silence and moving to another city right now is not in the cards.

Not with Natalie still being here.

After I make the quick call, I head back to my apartment and wait, pacing around the living room. Steve's in his room, talking to someone in a game, so I don't interrupt. Besides, I'm so confused myself that I don't have time to explain. Once my pickup time is close, I head to the balcony to watch for cars. At least I can see the parking lot from here.

The black Mercedes pulls in fifteen minutes later, right on the dot. I walk down and wave, and the drivers' side window goes down a bit to reveal a young guy with dark hair and a square jaw.

"It's Don," he says with a grin.

"Oh," I say, relieved. I haven't seen him or Matt without their suits on before.

For now.

Because if Salvos wants an inventor that bad, they're going to have to work with me. And I'm nervous about making demands. Nervous, and desperate.

If they don't cooperate, I lose nothing, I think.

I get into the back of the car. Candi's not in the vehicle this time. Don drives me back to the Salvos office/apartment building without saying much, and then Candi's waiting in the underground garage, cute as ever. Today she's wearing a navy blue suit that contrasts with her red hair and pale skin.

It is one hundred percent a trap.

She opens the back door for me. "So, you changed your mind?" Her green eyes flash.

"I'll cut to it," I say as soon as I'm out of the car. "I know you guys need someone who does mob traps and auto farms, but I need to get paid for being a beta tester. A free apartment is great, but my sister is about to have major medical bills and she's on the verge of losing her job. Also, I have bills I have to pay, and I can't hold down another job and do this at the same time." I square my shoulders as I speak, letting Candi know that I mean business. While I don't really know her, she seems like the type who will try to make it happen. Then I turn to Don. "How do you manage it?"

"I do gaming vids full time already," he says. "And I beta test this secret game on the side."

I shouldn't be surprised at that fact, but I am surprised Don gave me an answer at all with all the secretive stuff going on. If Don is a streamer, a successful one, money won't be an issue for him. But that gives me ammo for what I say next. "So is everyone here except for me already getting paid outside of this for doing gaming full time?"

Candi swallows. I'm laying the pressure on. It would make sense for Salvos to approach well-known streamers for a closed beta. That's the way it works in the gaming world. And that would explain why they're not paying people to do it.

"The people we've brought on are already established. Yes," Candi says, but instead of putting up a wall, she grins a little like she wants me to continue.

"Well, I'm not, so my circumstance is different. It's unfair to me to ask me to work for free."

"Don't you have another job? You can easily juggle both, if you're used to gaming in your free time anyway," Candi says. But she maintains that question in her eyes. She wants me to say I'm staying on.

I wave her aside, leaving Don to lock up the car. I don't speak until we're near the door to the stairwell and elevator. "I lost my job today at the call center. They canned me for being late the other night. Oh, and because I told a customer how to escape their cycle of terror. You should have expected that first part."

Candi bites her lip. "I am sorry about that. But we were confident that you would take the offer."

"Without having a paying job to help me?" *That* part ticks me off.

"Well, it's the protocol that corporate wants." Candi leans close and whispers in my ear as if there's a spy next to us, using an invisibility cloak. "Again, I'm sorry. I'll see what I can do for you." She looks away and blinks.

I've laid on the guilt.

And I almost feel bad about it.

"Follow me," Candi says, raising her voice again.

Please, don't let me be a charity case, I think as we go up the elevator and then through the testing room. Tonight, three players are immersed in the mystery game, all suited and mysterious, and one seems to be chopping wood in front of him judging from his motions. Another is looking downward as if into a pit.

Candi walks faster through the gray room, waving me along, and we come to a T-junction where she takes a right. Now we're in an office hallway with a faint musty smell. Doors line the walls and we enter the second to last one.

It's a lounge with leather furniture and lush carpet that looks as if it belongs in the seventies. It's empty but there's a minibar on one side of the room and glass furniture. No television, though, and no gaming systems. A disco ball hangs from the ceiling and a retro record player waits in the corner.

"This place is pretty cool," I say.

"Anthony's a fan of the seventies," Candi says. "Have a seat. This isn't usual protocol but I'll see if I can get something for you. Mike, you're in demand, and you're a different case, so I just might be able to make it work." She winks as she moves back to the door before exiting the room. I listen as she steps into the room right across the hall. The door squeaks as it swings back, but I don't hear a click.

I stand there like a moron and want to slap myself. Then I mull over Candi's words as I sit down, digging my fingers into the leather of the couch. She's left the lounge door partly open. And, most likely, the door on the other end of the hall, too.

Is that an invitation?

It's obvious she's trying to make things right. As soon as the thought hits me, I get up. I'm not sitting here while she discusses my future. I move to the lounge door, listening to the faint sound of her cell phone ringing someone in the other room.

Bingo. Candi hasn't moved far away at all.

"Anthony? Yes, looking for that Anthony Anton." A long pause follows. "Oh, he's on his jet? That's fine if I can talk to an assistant, so long as it's fine with Anton." She goes silent again. "Hi, Miriam. Is it true that the CEO still wants a mob grinder and auto farm specialist on the closed beta?"

Specialist? I hold back a snort. Corporations have to find boring names for everything.

"Yes. I have Mike Wattles here. He's interested in Project 93. But his situation isn't like that of the other streamers. He needs pay to participate in this program. You see, he's between jobs, and if he takes the offer without having a source of income, job hunting will get in the way. Also, his sister is sick and needs help with medical bills. And he is a *very* good player. I promise that. I say it's a small price to pay for testing the finer aspects."

I grip the door frame.

"Great. So Anton's still interested. No, I don't think you'll get in trouble," Candi says. "Thank you so much, Miriam. Let Anton know and send it over as soon as you can."

My heart leaps.

Is this really happening?

Scrambling back to my seat, I wait, and Candi opens the door a moment later, grinning.

"Guess what?" she says, dropping that professional disguise. "You're on. Or should I say, you're probably *hired.* Before you sign the contract, it's standard for new team members to test Project 93."

CHAPTER EIGHT

Excitement bubbles into my chest as I follow Candi to the testing room. I haven't seen any paperwork or signed anything yet, and I'm anxious about that part because I know that letting me preview this Project 93 game is a move meant to sway me. Creationist is great but no company is going to give stuff out for free. Salvos will expect something out of me in return.

I hope that that *something* is just my performance.

When we reach the testing room, two players are still swinging at invisible obstacles or monsters in their glass boxes, illuminated by the blue lights. Don is waiting in plainclothes with a bunch of those suits slung over his big arm. Makes sense. No one handed me a form for me to fill out with my clothing size.

I take a breath to calm myself. This game, knowing Salvos, is probably something like Creationist.

"What should I expect?" I ask.

"I cannot say," Candi says, but she grins as if I'm in for some kind of joke. "You'll enjoy it."

"Going in blind, huh?" I nod to Don.

"Take your pick. I'm not going to stand here and assess you." Then he holds up his arm.

He's got a few of the suits dangling off his arm, minus helmets and gloves. Considering that they've all got those plastic-looking black pads on them, I'm guessing they're heavy. Don's patient as I sift through them. Turns out there's five suits. I grab the one with the tallest, skinniest pants, well aware that Candi's watching.

"Where do I change?"

"Over there," Don says, nodding to the side of the testing room. "Helmets and gloves are in there. All get sanitized every night. Once you're in your battle gear, brace yourself for the Salvos Simulator."

"Great," I say, pulse hammering. I'm nervous. In front of Candi. Awesome. "And don't worry. If I stay on, I'll push this game to the limits and test every mechanic I can."

Candi grins.

I eye an empty glass box and the rollerballs that make up the floor. My palms sweat. I'm sure there's a reason for making me go in blind. In Creationist, there's little I haven't exploited yet. I've tried every mob farm out there and invented some of my own. I've built every auto farm and turned every Monster Fort into a grinder to suit my own needs. I've always known what to do.

For this game, I'm a complete noob.

I go into the changing room, which turns out to be behind a door that's between two Salvos Simulators. It's a small room bathed in that same blue light, with shelves of helmets and the black gloves, plus pairs of black boots lined up on the floor. And lockers. I read the name stickers on the fronts. *Candi. Don. Matt. Val. Liz. Kevin.* Two lockers are blank, and I take the second the last one, stashing my clothes inside.

The suit fits me fine and the plastic pads press against everything that's not a joint or crease. This suit is like nothing I've ever worn. The pads feel like static on contact with my skin, as if they're electrifying me, but they're not uncomfortable. Just weird. And unlike my Virtual World Helmet back at home. The boots bathe my feet in that same sensation, and the gloves make every nerve in my hands dance.

"To have a good time, press the space bar," I joke to myself.

What am I getting into?

Now for the helmet.

I'm a bit nervous about putting it on, but I grab one off the shelf and slip it over my head. The same electric sensation surrounds my skull as it slips into place, and a brief light flashes behind my eyelids when I blink. But it's gone a moment later.

I feel as if I'm wired into this thing. What kind of technology does Salvos have here?

At least I can see through the smooth, tinted glass of the visor and somehow I can breathe with a faint whooshing sound. And then I unlock the door with my gloves, which are surprisingly versatile, almost like a second skin.

Candi and Don are waiting in the testing room. As I step out, the tingling dies down. Maybe the blue light has something to do with how these suits work.

"So," I said, my own voice sounding too loud in my ears. "Will this VR helmet ever have recording capabilities?" I haven't even tested Project 93 yet and I'm wondering about what opportunities this can offer.

Candi's waiting by one of the Salvos Simulator boxes with the door open. "Your helmet does have those capabilities, but for the purposes of monitoring your progress. Player-controlled recording functions will come later, along with other vital controls. For now, you need to trust us. You understand what beta testing entails, right?"

"I do. Test the game to the hilt and report back on any bugs and balance issues."

"Right."

"You're serious that I'm going in completely blind."

"I doubt someone like you will have much trouble once you've got the hang of how Project 93 works," Candi says, opening the glass door of an empty Simulator for me. "You have two real life hours."

Whoa. Don just awkwardly steps back while I get into the Simulator and catch my footing on the floor of marble-sized roller balls. They depress a little as I walk on them, making my step feel natural. Cool. The floor here is much bigger than the platform I've got at home. Enough to break into a full run, maybe, without ever hitting the walls. Despite being in a box, I don't feel as if I'm enclosed. The air is still and cool and the blue light shines down on me, casting a calming glow.

But being under that strange blue light again makes my suit tingle.

"What's going to happen now?" I ask.

"Watch out for the transition period," Candi says from behind me. "Logging in is automatic."

"The what?"

A loud buzzing fills my head, seizing me in place, and the plastic pieces of my suit, including the chest piece, increase their tempo. I jolt as the glass on my helmet turns completely black. A falling sensation as if I'm on a roller coaster socks me. I can't feel the floor. I'm floating in a black, endless space.

No.

I'm free falling.

A few choice words escape me. If Candi's standing nearby, I can't hear her. And if this is part of the beta test—

I land on my back with a painless *thud* as a blur of color fills my vision.

My breath shoots out of me as the tingling vanishes. I blink, no longer encased in, well, anything. A morning sky, complete with pale orange light that's rapidly shifting to blue, stretches overhead. A bit of wind blows against my face. Leaves rustle. I inhale and smell a bit of grass. A strange pressure on my back lets me know that I'm lying on top of something crumpled.

"Candi?" I ask, craning my neck back so I'm looking at what I think is the back of the Salvos Simulator. "Whoa."

I'm not in a glass box with roller balls at all, but lying on a flat landscape that looks like a cross between a plain of short grass and a forest. The tops of a few trees lower into my upside-down vision. I turn my head back to normal, letting my vision pan over the sky. A few clouds drift overhead, floating towards a rising sun that looks like a cartoon pentagon and not an actual ball of burning gas. The transparent, pixelated clouds have the same straight lines, forming triangular points where curves should be.

"I'm in the game." No title screen. No loading screen hints. The VR suit and the Simulator have just thrown me into a whole new reality.

Project 93.

Then I do let out a few choice words, but in awe instead of sickness. My nausea's gone. Despite the throwback graphics that tell me I'm obviously not in Kansas anymore, everything else feels like the real deal. The pressure of the ground is making my butt go numb. With each breath I can smell the outdoors. Leaves rustle in the wind. And now I know why Salvos Corporation wants to keep this creation—this place—top secret.

This isn't virtual reality.

It's a whole new reality, period.

I haven't even gotten up and I'm already impressed.

I reach up to the sky, wiggling my fingers. I'm shocked to see that my hand isn't a long block with a series of block fingers like it is in Creationist, but an actual hand. Sure, my fingers are long triangles with points, and there are no real curves in my joints, but I've got a hand and I can feel my fingers wiggling and the air moving against my skin.

And I even still have that mole on my ring finger that I do in real life, in the form of a pixel.

I'm also wearing a cartoonish, cloth, brown suit with leather pads on my forearms, right where the plastic ones are on my actual Salvos VR suit. Again, no curves. I'm in a world of straight lines.

Then I do my first test and touch my face, expecting to feel the glass mask of my helmet before my hand reaches me.

Nope. My fingers land on my nose, chilly from the wind.

Impressive. Just impressive. This feels like Creationist, but it doesn't.

I push myself into a sitting position, listening to the grass under me rustle. My first impression turns out to be true. I'm in area made of short, pale green grass and scattered trees. While some of the trees are taller than others, they have a strange uniform look. Their trunks form no curves either—they're basically pentagons themselves—and each trunk has a repeating bark texture, maybe 64-bit. The leaves? Same story, except they're transparent.

Long story short: everything here is made of pentagons.

And it's got a strange charm.

Salvos could have done realistic graphics, easily, but I like this. If the mechanics are as awesome as I hope, this game *is* going to take the world by storm.

Another tingle sweeps over me. I'm a kid playing Creationist for the first time all over again.

Get up, Mike. I can't just sit here when there's a world to explore.

CHAPTER NINE

I push myself off the ground, amazed at how my act compares to the real thing. I can feel my muscles stretching, the short, springy grass under my palm, and my black boots scraping against the ground.

"Get your bearings, Mike. Figure out how to play," I say to myself. I don't know if this is a horror game, a game full of aliens, or something else entirely. The first thing I need to do is check out the area.

Something tan walks between the trees ahead and I jump at the sight of the figure about a hundred feet away. Then I lean closer, squint, and see that it's a goat. A goat with a body and horns made of straight lines and points. It looks like something I'd see in Creationist but not quite. "Okay. So unless goats can eat you here, this doesn't seem to be a horror game." Creationist had sprawling, dark forests, swamps, and wastelands. I let out a breath, remembering that I have no audience except for Salvos Corporation. All talking will be to myself.

The goat jumps up and down stupidly, legs still straight, and makes whatever sound a goat makes. Then it stops, and without an animation for the transition, it tilts its head down to the grass, probably chewing.

"A peaceful mob, then. Probably a food source or a garbage disposal." Or neutral.

I turn away and walk across the short grass, marveling at how real it feels. The pentagon sun has risen a bit more. Day seems to be going past quickly and I'm guessing it might be done in an hour. If this game is anything like Creationist, night is going to bring trouble, and being armed with just my fists isn't the way I want to face it. Standing here with my jaw down could lead to me standing under the stars with my pants down.

"Okay. Get oriented, Wattleman," I tell myself, tapping myself on the chest. My chest plate, leather in this world, makes a faint thud.

I'm rewarded with four status bars in rows of two, which appear at the bottom of my vision, floating in midair. The top left bar is green, with a red heart beside it. Health. The one in the lower left corner is yellow with a sandwich beside it. A food bar. The bar on the upper right is empty but has a gray, cartoon helmet. Armor. And despite my leather plates, I have none. Apparently this brown uniform doesn't provide any armor. And the bottom right bar is blue, full, and features a set of three bubbles. Oxygen, maybe. So drowning must be a thing here.

I tap my chest again, dismissing the status bars. "Well, that's settled."

Now it's time to explore the area and see what I can do.

Walking through the trees, I leave my spawn point behind. So far, this area seems pretty uniform, with the trees all being the same type and the pixelated grass the same bright green color. As I walk, more land renders into existence maybe two hundred feet ahead of me, chunk by chunk.

Something quacks far to my right, but the sight of a tall cliff suddenly popping into existence ahead makes me stop in my tracks.

The cliff rises a hundred feet above the forest, with more of the trees, hazy from this distance, growing from the top. The wall itself is made of light gray stone with dirt on top. The cliff's so wide that I can't see either end of it anywhere.

"That's cool." As I get closer, I notice a spot in the stone with rusty greenish splotches. Some type of ore, maybe even copper. Yeah, I've got no chance at getting it yet, though it would be cool to scale the cliff and get a view of the area or maybe even build a base there.

I eye the sun. It's the equivalent of nine in the morning by now. Scaling the cliff will have to wait.

"Stay alive, Mike." I seem safe for the moment, so I've got to test some things. I jump to test that—it seems I have a higher jump than in real life, maybe three feet, the height of each pentagon that makes up the tree trunks. Useful. Then I tap myself on the left shoulder, and a tall, narrow box appears before me with a wooden frame, a background that matches the bark texture, and a thin outline of a body. A box for equipping armor, probably. I tap again to dismiss it.

Tapping my right shoulder does nothing. Then I tap my back, feeling a deflated backpack there before another, much larger box pops into my vision, obstructing my view of the cliff.

"My inventory." This box has the same wooden frame and background as the armor one and shows an empty hotbar with six mini-boxes at the bottom. A bigger inventory with five rows of ten boxes stands empty. Generous. A 3x3 tab hangs off the right of the frame and though it's not labeled, I assume it must be for crafting. So the recipes in this game might be more complicated than in Creationist, which only gives the player a 2x2 grid in their inventory.

I dismiss the inventory by hitting my backpack again and face some leaves on a nearby tree. The unseen duck quacks again so I search for it. I glimpse what appears to be sand mixed with pink and gray pixels—probably gravel—around a pond. A duck with triangular wings jumps up and down, flapping them like a moron. The water shimmers with pixels under the sunlight.

One thing at a time. I face the leaves and hold out my hand, highlighting them. They brighten a bit, letting me know I've selected their hitbox. So one thing has carried over from Creationist. "Thank you, Salvos. That's intuitive."

Then I slug them.

The leaves rustle for a bit but don't break. Then I try again, slugging them over and over, this time maintaining the motion. The rustling continues until the polygon of leaves breaks in a mini explosion of green.

Three items rest on the ground, dropped from the leaves, lying flat against the grass and made of pixels. Two sticks, both identical with the bark texture, and a small, shrunken clod of leaves. I stand over them, but they don't automatically zip into my inventory, so I tap each item and watch it vanish with a faint *plork* sound.

"Bingo." I can pick stuff up now.

I open my inventory (backpack tap again) to see the sticks in one slot, which have stacked and now have a number 2 in the corner of their box. The leaves are there too, with a 1, and I lift my pointed finger and highlight that box as I hover over it. A tooltip appears, rimmed in the wood texture. *Common Leaves.* Then *Common Stick.*

I like the mechanics of picking up items, so far. No more cramped inventories full of junk. Creationist's items automatically zipped into a player's inventory whenever items were on the ground and I was constantly throwing stuff out. Okay, so this mechanic might be a pain when I need to pick up a ton of building blocks or in the heat of battle, but for now it works.

I collect more Common Sticks and Common Leaves until I have twenty of each. Common Sticks are probably needed for making tools and weapons. Once I've decimated the poor tree down to its trunk with my savage punches, I decide to put it out of its misery and slug the polygon trunk with my fist instead.

Pressure slams into my knuckles and grips my forearm and my view flashes with faint red at the edges. My status bars appear in my vision and I see that my green health bar has depleted a tiny sliver. Then the bars vanish.

"Fine, fine. That was stupid." I shake my hand as the pressure vanishes. Of course breaking a tree trunk by punching it doesn't make sense. What kind of game would allow that? "A hatchet, saw, or axe it is."

But my problem is, how?

"Mike, you can solve this issue." If this game is like Creationist, the first step will be to make tools and something useful for defending myself. Then I can worry about inventions. "Common Sticks can make a handle. But unless you want an axe with a leaf blade, look around."

Blade, blade. My mind goes to the gravel sand I saw back at that pond, so I head back that way. The duck has de-spawned. "I need something I can get with my bare hands. Some crappy first tier material. Die, sand!"

And I start punching.

At least the sand is soft, even though I can feel the gravel in it, and it breaks without much effort, dropping small sprites of itself. But my hope that it'll drop a flint or arrowhead is dashed after I pick it all up and check my inventory.

Rocky Sand. That really helps.

"I should be getting something," I mutter, breaking a few more of the Rocky Sand and earning a small waterfall from the pond. The pixelated, cold water pushes me back and into the hole I've made, and as I watch, the whole pond lowers as water fills my hole. A chill wraps around my torso as I stand waist-deep in it. I pull myself out, and a brief storm of water particles bursts to life around me before vanishing.

"So water is realistic in this game," I mutter. Not useful for mob traps, then. Back in Creationist, I could place blocks of water that flowed but never ran out.

I eye the pentagon in the sky. *Mike Wattles stands under the high noon sun, with Rocky Sand and Common Sticks to his name.* That'll sure intimidate a monster.

I've got to get a move on.

Running back towards my spawn point, I leave the cliff behind and scan the ground for more resources. Everything looks the same in this area. I punch to death some tall grass, which breaks with a loud rustle. My prize? A tan squiggly thing lying on the ground.

I pick it up.

And hallelujah—it's a Plant Strand.

"Okay. That might be useful," I say, hope filling my chest. "Break the tall grass." So I move on to killing the lawn for a bit. But I get some Plant Strands, twenty of them.

"Achievement get," I mutter even though I have no audience. "Primitive Lawnmower."

Now what?

I spot a few polygon flowers scattered around the trees, mostly in clusters, a few orange and yellow ones. I break them too, and earn a few more Plant Strands. What use flowers have other than decoration, I don't know yet, but I'll keep them for now.

I open my inventory and realize that like in Creationist, I can use my finger to slide the items around. I try a few combinations of Common Sticks and Plant Strands in my 3 x 3 Crafting Tab, but get nothing in the output box I realize is just underneath the tab for the first time. Then I try combining just Plant Strands on the grid to see what I get, and it turns out that combining four, in any arrangement, gets me a single Plant Twine, a thick-looking greenish tan rope. I make a bunch more until I have six. Yes. Tool-making material for sure. At least the start of this game is intuitive without walking you through every step, like later versions of Creationist did once it got popular.

Now, to find the final tool ingredient. Because unless I want a butterfly net, I can't make anything else with what I've got.

"And there aren't even any butterflies," I mutter.

I keep walking, circling around spawn. This whole biome looks to be a forest with the trees growing pretty far apart. Pretty uniform. I spot a few big holes that seem to lead into caves or underground tunnels. I find nothing more promising than Rocky Sand, of which there are a few random, flat patches here and there.

But finally, after I've gone some distance from the cliff, the ground slopes downward in a series of diagonal lines and polygons, and down the hill stand trees with whitish tan trunks and barely any leaves. More water stretches out, but unlike the happy little pond I found a few minutes ago, this water is greenish and dark.

"A swamp biome. This looks welcoming," I say, eyeing the dead trees, some of which are growing out of the water.

The air chills as I walk downhill, eyeing the dark grass and listening to the squishing sound my footsteps make. Collecting a few of the ground blocks here yields me Damp Soil, which is dark and seems laced with green moss, judging from the faint green pixels both the sprites and the boxes themselves have. I keep digging downward with my fist, forming disorganized steps, hoping to find some stone shards or something I can harvest. Hey, I can't walk in circles forever.

Underneath a few Damp Soil layers, I find a new material, something darker than the Damp Soil that has black and gray spots.

"What the heck is this?"

I start hitting it with my hand, and it feels dry to my shock, but the mystery material remains in place even though I don't take damage. It makes a sound like breaking dirt, not stone, and I give up after ten seconds. I can't harvest this by hand, so I'll leave it for now.

"Frustrating," I mutter, pulling up my inventory again. I eye my prizes so far. There must be one more component needed to make some kind of tool. I'm guessing a shovel and hatchet are my next steps. The first two steps make sense. The third? No beans.

I'm missing *something.*

Then with my inventory still floating in front of me, I lift my hand and highlight each item with my finger. Nothing appears as I hover over Common Soil. I tap it once, and my inventory vanishes. A full 3D pentagon of Common Soil has appeared in my right hand.

"Yay. I've just equipped the ultimate noob weapon."

I can highlight the grass pieces around me and know I can place this dirt, but I don't. At least my left hand is free to tap my backpack. I can put the dirt back in my inventory by shoving it at the desired box.

Then I figure out that I can put stuff in my six-slot hotbar with two quick taps. Now that there's stuff in it, my hotbar remains at the bottom of my vision when I close my inventory—handy—but I've still just got some dirt, Plant Twine, and Common Sticks. I can equip stuff on the fly by highlighting, though, which is nice.

Then I open my inventory again and try hovering my finger over a random item. After a few seconds, an expanded tooltip appears beside the dirt.

Common Soil

Resistance: 1

Fall Damage: -1

Gravity: 0

Speed: 0

"Aha! That's going to make things easier. We might have clues. We're in familiar territory, folks."

In Creationist, items had properties assigned in the code, which I studied in detail to make my mob farms. This game might be the same, coming from the same makers.

I'm assuming that Resistance is a regular scale that runs from 1 to whatever, with the higher numbers meaning that the resource is harder to break or requires higher tier tools. 1 must mean I can break the resource with my hand.

The -1 to Fall Damage must mean that landing on Common Soil from a good height is slightly less damaging than landing on something with a Fall Damage of 0 or higher. Good to know.

Gravity and Refinable, I'm assuming, are just yes and no answers. I'll figure out Gravity later. In cases like this, zero typically means "no" while 1 means "yes." So Common Soil probably can't be turned into anything else and might not be affected by gravity, making it a possible roof material that won't fall on me and deal suffocation damage.

I check the other resources I've found. The flowers, I'm shocked, are Refinable (1) but the Plant Strands aren't. I'm confused for a bit. Refinable must mean that an item can be turned into something else entirely rather than just being part of some crafting recipe. "Okay. I've got it."

And then I check the Rocky Sand.

And I see what I was hoping for.

Refinable: 1.

Hope surges through me but quickly dies when I see that the glowing pentagon, now on the other side of my inventory box, is sinking towards the horizon. It appears to be a few hours past noon.

I'm running out of time. Tension crawls into my shoulders.

I place the Rocky Sand into my Crafting Tab. Nothing. Seriously? Do I need another tool to refine the Rocky Sand? Maybe another block? I sigh. Rocky Sand offers the best bet for getting the last crafting ingredient for a tool. Why can't I just pull something useful out of it? Maybe my hands are considered too clumsy to sift—

Can I make something to sift the Rocky Sand?

I sit down on the dark grass of the swamp's edge, still with my inventory open...and eye my Plant Twine and Sticks.

And there, ladies and gentlemen, is the sound of a light bulb clicking on.

I slide two sticks into my Crafting Tab and then three Plant Twine, putting them in the arrangement that makes the most sense, but nothing appears in the output. Then I try four sticks, with two columns on either side of the grid, and three Plant Twine in the top row.

And lo and behold, something that looks like, well, a pixelated sifter on four legs appears in my output. I tap it and it zooms into my inventory.

Yes. It's a Sifter. Simple as that.

I put it back in my Crafting Grid and place the Rocky Sand above it, but nothing happens. Then I equip the Sifter.

It feels big and awkward in my hand at full size. The Sifter is just four crude wooden legs and a net of Plant Twine. With my gaze I highlight a patch of flat ground, since I'm still on the slope that goes down to the swampy area. Then I place the Sifter by shoving it at where I want it to go.

With a faint *thump,* it appears there.

And to sift, it turns out, I just need to place my Rocky Sand on top of the Sifter. I equip the stack of it, and though one piece of Rocky Sand appears in my hand at a time, every time I place one on the Sifter, the next on in the stack appears in my hand. Convenient. And the Sifter works as fast as I can place. The sound of falling sand fills the air as each pentagon of the stuff vanishes.

And two things happen.

Blocks that look like pure sand appear under the Sifter.

And so do some shining gray shards.

Heart racing with victory and excitement, I pick them all up.

Flint Shard. Eighteen of them, and just as much Pure Sand.

Another tingle of victory surges up my spine.

"I'm figuring out this game."

And then a horrific, drawn-out sound echoes from not far below me at all.

Low and guttural, I can only describe the noise as an inhuman *sclorc* combined with an sucking sound. I jump, looking down, but solid, damp ground spreads out below me. The sound's coming from somewhere below the dark mystery material I can't yet break.

The sound comes again, a bit louder. I also detect faint, wet footsteps. Yes. Whatever's making it is below me, probably in some underground room or cavity. A shudder replaces my tingle of victory.

There are bad things in this world, things that lurk in the dark.

And the pentagon sun is getting very close to the horizon.

CHAPTER TEN

Time to hustle.

The weird sound repeats, getting fainter as whatever's below my feet moves away, probably through a cavern or tunnel. But I don't stop to track the sound. If I don't get somewhere safe, and quick, then—

"That thing down there is going to pop onto the surface and eat my face."

And with this realism thing going on, that's not an experience I look forward to.

There's also my other problem. Acting like a noob won't get me hired by Salvos. Candi's confirmed that they're watching.

I break the Sifter with my hand (thankfully the Resistance is only 1) and it shrinks, falls to the ground, and pops into my inventory when I poke it. Then I turn away. "Shelter. Shelter. Even a pile of rocks will work."

The sky's turning orange on the horizon.

And so is the pentagon sun.

Trees spread out uphill in the scattered woods area, where I know the land is open all around except for those holes in the ground. And venturing into one of those right now isn't an option, mainly because underground is where that sound is.

I run along the bottom of the hill, staying between it and the swamp water, huffing and puffing as I search for shelter. The dead trees? Nope. The first ranged enemy will take me out and I don't like the thought of getting treed by a ring of hostile mobs. "Come on, land. Cooperate with me here."

The horizon goes pink. The light level's dropping by the minute. Night falls quickly here, within just a few minutes. Yikes.

An indent in the hill meets my eye, and I peek in to see a shallow cave that goes back maybe twenty feet. Thankfully, I spot no mobs, eat-your-face or otherwise, and dive inside.

It's going to be a long night.

The cave floor is stone and slopes down a few feet. Not enough protection. I don't know if fires are possible in this game, but I don't have time to sit and figure it out.

That opening to the outside is a problem.

I open my inventory to find a few Common Dirt, my Common Leaves, and Common Sticks. Awesome. Quickly I equip the Common Dirt, feeling like the total noob I am, and I boldly march to the cave entrance with dirt in hand. Then I place a few chunks of it along the bottom in the same manner I placed the Sifter. Each dirt chunk comes up to my waist once placed. Stuff returns to its original size when placed. Good.

But it smells like, well, dirt.

Could be worse.

Full night has almost fallen by the time I finish the bottom row of my barrier (six 3ft x 3ft dirt chunks in a row.) That still leaves a nice view of the swampy lake that's opposite me, and I'm out of Common Dirt so I equip the Pure Sand next.

And then I learn the meaning of Gravity in this game.

Each time I place the Pure Sand, it slides right off the dirt wall and slides either downhill towards the lake, or down the slope of my cave. Yeah, it stays in pentagon form as it does, but it's still frustrating.

"Well, that's useful," I shout, tension rising up my spine.

So I equip the Common Leaves next and place them, forming a wall between me and the outdoors. The leaves are the same story as the dirt. When I place them with a rustling sound, they appear in their original sizes.

"Good job, Mike," I say. "You're going to survive until daybreak." Was day here about a real-life hour? Great. That means night could be the same.

Then I see Problem Number Two.

I can see through the wall of Common Leaves.

And already the world has gone into *I'm Gonna Kill You Mode.*

A weird green light shimmers above the lake in the distance. Particles fall off the floating spiral. Swamp gas, maybe. Or some hostile mob. And two other tall, lanky figures bounce up and down in the water, treading it.

They're both too tall to be human and too thin. But their heads are bulbous.

I feel really safe right now. (Insert sarcasm.)

"Okay, Mike. You're in here for the night," I mutter, backing away from my flimsy leaf wall and towards the back of the cave. "Craft something. Keep your brain occupied. Just don't make noise." I bring up my inventory and Crafting Tab by touching my backpack. At least I can still see my inventory box in full light and color.

And *phew*—I grabbed the Flint Shards.

"Distraction time. Just ignore the monsters. They can hang out there and talk about last night's *Game of Royals* episode." Then I shut up because I'm making noise. I go to work making various arrangements on the grid with the Flint Shards, Common Sticks, and the Plant Twine. Crafting will be similar to what I did for the Sifter—intuitive but not *too* intuitive.

After a few tries, I'm rewarded with something in the output that looks like a crude hatchet, with the gray, shiny blade tied to a stick by the Plant Twine. I tap the output and the tool zips into my inventory, like the Sifter did.

I highlight it and wait for the expanded tooltip.

Flint Hatchet
Strength: 2
Attack: 4
Speed: 3
Health: 150/150

Calories: -2

"Excellent." I equip it with the single tap and my inventory vanishes. Though I can't see it in the dark, I can feel that I'm holding a wooden handle that threatens a splinter with every movement. I swing it, satisfied at the *whoosh* it makes. The stats have told me it's a weapon as well as a tool. Strength must be its ability to break items, probably items with a Resistance of 2. Calories must be how much hungrier I'll get per swing.

Sclorc.

My heart leaps into my throat and something makes a repeated splashing sound in the lake. Not the distant side of the lake, but at the shore. Maybe, even, just thirty feet away.

I lean closer to the leaf wall, but it's so dark now I can only see some small pentagon stars in the sky, slowly moving overhead, and that green particle swamp gas thing in the distance. It floats around aimlessly, seeming to stay over where I think the water is.

Than another *sclorc* sound follows...and it's very close. To my right. Already well onto land.

I back off, raising my Flint Hatchet.

"Okay. This is a horror game," I hiss.

The sound follows and it seems whatever is walking around is right above me. Squishy footsteps come after that, slow and dragging. Then they fade in the direction of the scattered woods area.

"Great." I scratch my head in the silent break, but to my shock, another wooden pane appears before me. It looks like my inventory and has the same bark texture for the background, but there's a bunch of text on it.

DAY 1
LIGHT: 2
FACING: SOUTH-SOUTHEAST

BIOME: NORTHERN SWAMP [BORDER]
TEMPERATURE: 45
HUMIDITY: 55
ELEVATION: 10
HOSTILITY: 70

More info. I take in what I'm reading and force myself to calm down. I've found something else important. Many people would ignore this stuff, but to me it's gold.

Certain mobs could have rules for spawning, like needing a certain biome, temperature, or elevation, and using this screen will be useful for farming certain mobs. Light levels will probably be important too.

And...hostility?

I've never seen that stat in any sandbox game before.

Assuming zero means no hostile mobs spawn and 100 means you'd better drop your inventory and give up now, I'm assuming that 70 is not good.

Sclorc.

I hit the top of my head again, dismissing the new screen. Gross, wet footsteps approach from above, and then a dark figure drops in front of my leaf barrier with a disgusting, mushy sound. Long, lanky limbs claw at my leaves, which rustle as the creature slowly pushes its way through.

My heart sinks and I jump.

Oh no.

Oh, yes.

The tall monster with the bulbous head is pushing through my leaves. It's already stepped up onto the Common Soil layer.

The First Deadly Sin of Salvosera. Thou shall not use leaves as a wall.

The Common Leaves must have a Speed score of minus ten or something. Now isn't the time to think of how I can use that. "Stay alive, Mike." If punching a tree trunk almost hurt, what's this thing going to do?

I lift my Flint Hatchet, barely able to see its outline against the stars.

And then, lo and behold, the creature drops off the dirt layer, having pushed all the way into my cave. It lifts one arm at me. My heart hammers and my sweaty palms almost make me drop my weapon.

Sclorc.

I swing. "Get out of here!"

The monster makes a sound between a hiccup and a scream as my Flint Hatchet makes a sickening thump against its flesh. Pressure runs up my arm, but my health's fine. Bingo!

But the monster doesn't flinch or retreat like a normal being.

And now, more *sclorcs* sound in the distance and I fear my enemy has just called backup.

I swing again to be rewarded with another thump, but then something long and lanky swings at me from the left, and then a strong, greasy hand strikes me on the side and my view flashes redder than it did when I punched the tree. The pressure in my side is immense. My health bar rises into my vision, now down a full quarter. Crap. The green bar slowly regenerates, but my Calories bar shrinks in tandem with it.

I swing two more times, accidentally breaking some Common Leaves. A window. Just what I need. But I strike the mostly-unseen monster, glimpsing bluish-green flesh in the starlight, before it makes one final-sounding weak hiccup and falls to the cave floor and explodes into dark gray particles.

I replace the missing leaves which have dropped as items on my side of the barrier, aware I've got no more in my inventory. Worse, the *sclorcs* are still sounding outside. How far away? Maybe this monster has dropped something I can use to defend myself.

Yes. I can faintly see something on the cave floor, a dark splotch and what appears to be a white line, and I lean down and tap the mob drops to collect them. *Plork.* When I check my inventory for my prize, I find a greenish-blue chunk of what looks like rotten meat. Putrid Flesh. Awesome. And a Bone. Yet despite that, my stomach rumbles.

I'm actually feeling hungry in the game.

I pull up my health bar by tapping my chest and find that I'm halfway healed from my injury, but my Calories bar has just depleted by a full quarter. As I watch, my red Health bar climbs slower and slower and then stops. The mechanic makes sense, as I'm assuming a full stomach will heal better than an empty one.

I'm hoping the Putrid Flesh isn't on the menu. Then again, what game would want players to eat something like that? But I check it out in my inventory and hover for the tooltip, praying during the three-second wait.

Putrid Flesh
Refinable: 1
Edible: 0
Fuel: 0

"Prayer answered," I say.
But there's no time for relief.
Sclorc.
Sclorc.

Wet footsteps. Louder.

Sclorc.

I slap my backpack, which is now bulging a bit, to close my inventory.

Backup is here.

I bolt to the rear of the cave, putting my back against cold stone. The first pink light of dawn appears on the horizon, outlining the dead trees growing from the water, but does that make me feel better? Nope. Three dark figures appear before my leaf barrier. Rustling follows as they push through. The early morning glow gives me a view of what's pushing through my crappy barrier.

I'll vote for ghouls since zombies don't have claws, and these things are vaguely humanoid with blue-green, mottled skin and sunken faces with black eyes. None wear clothes. It's all featureless, seal-like skin with a pixilated shine. Their arms move in an inhuman up and down pattern as they push through the leaves, long legs unmoving, and towards me.

At least they don't stink. And I'm not suggesting to Salvos that they add that.

But I can't take comfort from that because I'll never take three of them at once. My chances of dying are probably ninety percent.

But still, I raise my hatchet as the pentagon sun rises behind them.

But then the monsters, all at once, begin to let out a cacophony of hiccup-screams. They flash reddish each time they do, indicating they're taking damage.

"What the—" I start.

Are the Common Leaves not such a dumb idea after all?

Or is it the daylight?

The daylight. One of the ghoul things makes it through the barrier, into the shade of my cave, and stops taking damage while its two buddies continue to struggle behind it. Both of them drop dead, and I swing at what I hope is a weakened monster. With a single thud, the last ghoul drops dead into a puff of smoke, leaving two Bones. Its buddies have also left gifts of Putrid Flesh and Bones.

I stand there, eyeing the rising sun.

I did it.

TheWattleman: 1. This New Game: 0.

And I already have my first invention idea.

But just as I lean down to pick up the mob drops, the world goes dark and I'm falling through a void. My time is up.

CHAPTER ELEVEN

"Hey! I was having fun!" I pull off my black helmet as soon as I realize I'm standing on a bunch of roller balls in the futuristic cop suit. I blink, shocked at the artificial blue light that surrounds me. An intense prickling sensation from the suit dies down from a storm to what it was when I left the changing room.

I turn to reorient myself. Yes. I'm back in the Salvos Simulator. And Candi's standing at the glass door she's holding open, an open laptop on the floor beside her.

"I'm really sorry," Candi says with a grimace. Then she lifts an eyebrow. "It's addictive, isn't it?"

"You've played? I...I almost died, but it was cool, and wow, my heart's still pounding. Creationist was scary when I first started playing, and this brought that whole feeling back by like, ten times."

"I see you met the Swamp Ghouls." She grins and motions me out. "Intermediate mob, actually. There's a Common type and then there's your friends."

"Why did you log me out?" I sound like a kid.

"Your two hours were up? Right now, players get so immersed in Salvosera that they have to be reminded to exit the game. The devs are working on adding reminders to the game like the real world time, but there's the issue of having those reminders break the experience, so the implementation hasn't come yet. So I had to cut you off."

"That was really two hours." I step out and adjust to standing on the regular floor again. Three other players are still deep in their experiences and I'm instantly jealous. That big guy in the suit over there might even be Don. "So the game's name is Salvosera."

"Yes."

"So I get to stay?" I hate that I sound like a drooling moron. What is Candi doing to me? I want to play that awesome game again. I already have an idea for a mob trap thanks to those Common Leaves. Already I want to experiment. "Trust me, I'll have tons of suggestions and praise."

Candi just offers that alluring smile. "I think you'll do well. You'll need to sign a contract before you continue. Anton's assistant had his lawyers draft one up while you were playing."

My heart sinks at the thought of perusing small print and trying to spot loopholes. *It's a trap!* "Do I get my own lawyer?" Sure, I know some stuff about law, but I'm rusty due to not finding a job in my field and due to it well, being pretty late at night. My adrenaline's wearing off and with it, I feel my eyes sagging.

"You can find one and have them look it over before you sign. They're okay with that." Candi frowns a bit as if remembering that I'm not a rich dude.

And I'm *not* okay with that.

Sinking back to reality, I go and change. Candi waits for me and when I come out of the changing room, I follow her through the gaming area and back into the seventies lounge. She tells me to have a seat and that they're faxing over the full contract. I do.

"Can I think this over and sign tomorrow?" I ask.

She follows me into the lounge as I sit on a bright yellow couch. "If you leave now, you'll still have to sign a non-disclosure agreement and an agreement not to come back. Drink?" She opens the mini bar.

Figures. But this hot chick is offering me a drink. But I force myself to shake my head while also wanting to slap myself for refusing. "I'm good. I want my mind clear when I look at this paperwork."

"Understandable. Maybe I shouldn't have offered." She grabs a bottle for herself and a small shot glass. Not professional, but at least it's after hours and I'm glad to see this place isn't formal. She sits on a bright blue couch. "So, Mike, while we're waiting for the fax, what do you think?"

I take a second to realize she's asking about the game. "Um, I think it's going to take off."

Candi laughs. "So do I." She sits on the other couch, crossing her legs. "Salvos has been developing this new game for a long time. Instead of just buying indie games and making them popular, they're trying to make their own thing."

Creationist was made by a small team of indie developers in Chicago over a decade ago, and when the game started taking off, Salvos came in and bought it, giving those guys a million each. "That's good that they're making their own games now."

"They can sure afford it," Candi says, "and afford to hire the best...never mind. You haven't signed anything yet, so I've got to clam up. Sorry."

"Look, I understand. Unless there's something shady in the contract, I'll sign. I mean, I could feel the wind on my face, and the grass under my feet, and when I tried to punch that tree trunk like a moron—"

"I know what you mean." Candi downs her shot.

A burning need to know how Salvos created an almost completely real experience almost bursts from me. This is some next level tech. "What was it, exactly? A hallucination of some sort?"

"Okay. All of reality happens in your brain," Candi says, tapping her head with both hands. "Even right now is just in your brain. I don't know exactly how they did it since I'm not a neuroscientist and I think they're stuffy, but they found some way to trick your senses into creating a new reality."

I laugh. "No crap. I got the idea that the suit was doing that."

"Only when turned on," Candi says. "So, what about the rest? The mechanics? I can't give you any spoilers, but I do need to collect your feedback. It's vital that the devs balance everything out."

"I liked that it was challenging but not impossible," I say. "That's how Creationist was when it first came out. You had to figure out what to do. Use your brain. Now when you log on, you get a bunch of on-screen instructions aimed at five year olds."

"Yes. It's all Explain Like I'm Five now."

"I mean, some players will get frustrated with it being that way, but someone always writes a wiki," I say. "So I think it'll work. Salvosera has that novelty Creationist used to have. And I like how everything has a mechanic you can find a way to exploit."

"Any...criticisms?" She seizes a tablet from the couch that I haven't noticed until now.

I think. "One thing so far. You have to pick up items one by one and that'll annoy people who are trying to collect lots of blocks at once. I mean, it's good that you don't get an inventory full of junk when you don't want it, but there should be an easy way to turn that feature on and off."

"That one, I agree with," Candi says. "Keep exploring, Mike. You'll find a way."

"I did like the info in the tooltips, though. Not too much of a clue but not too little. Made me feel smart."

Candi lifts an eyebrow. "Most people don't figure out the Sifter for a couple of in-game days, let alone the Flint Hatchet."

"You saw everything." I grab the edge of the couch.

"Yes." She taps the tablet with one orange painted fingernail. "We need to see what our players are up to. And that reminds me, I left my laptop in the testing room." She bites her lip, distracted.

"So no scratching my butt."

Great job, Mike. But Candi bursts out laughing.

I'm liking her more every second and I fear I'll sign that contract too fast.

"I'm sorry. I'm used to doing funny commentary," I say. Once she's done, I ask, "How are people going to afford this game? I can tell it needs a lot of space and equipment to run. I could never fit a Simulator in my living room."

"Salvos knows this, and it may be time to bring arcades back. They know people need an escape. Players just need to buy a Salvos Suit and a subscription to Salvosera. Gift cards will be available."

I gulp, thinking of how expensive the suits alone will be. "So, it'll start off being unaffordable for most people." Just testing this game—Salvosera—is a privilege that's among the stars, then.

Candi sighs. "That's the way of technology. But the price will come down."

I close my mouth, knowing I'm in no place to argue with a corporation's business model. Even if people have to travel to arcades to play this game, I know they won't be able to resist. "What about us live streamers? Those of us who make gaming videos?"

"Salvos is working on a plan to hire streamers to create additional buzz. They're going to want talent." She nods at me.

The room seems to expand. "I could eventually be—"

Candi's phone buzzes with a notification and she rises after looking at it. "The contract's here. Just rolled off the fax machine. Come on."

My head spins as she leads me to another room right across the hall, a meeting room complete with a shiny, dark table and leather chairs that mean business. Candi grabs the fax off the machine in the corner and puts it in front of me with a pen. "No rush. I'm sorry to put pressure on you like this. So take your time. I'm a night owl."

"So I can't take this home?" The small print is pale in places as if the machine needs some toner but I can at least read the print. The contract, to my relief, isn't very long, maybe ten pages or so. That's a shocker, considering it's got a non-disclosure agreement on the first page and conditions for my testing period on the rest.

"I'm afraid you can't. I'd let you but it's against corporate and I could get fired." Candi bites her lip. "But you can call a lawyer if you want. I know it's late."

An unspoken problem grows between us.

I'm poor. There's no way I can get a lawyer or find one willing to do pro bono, otherwise known as free, over a game. Or one willing to get mixed up with something top secret in an hours' notice without really good pay.

Candi and I stare at each other. Her green eyes offer a silent apology.

But she's done enough for me and pulled some strings, so I've got to give this an effort.

"I'll read every word of this slowly," I say, eyeing the clock on the wall. Despite this being a boring meeting room, the clock has bright green, neon-lit hands and numbers. Probably another one of Anton's touches. It's creeping up on midnight.

"I'll bring you some coffee," Candi says. "And no, that's not in my job description."

I read and sip on the awesome coffee she gets me from the lounge, and I'm not even a coffee guy. *Non-Disclosure Agreement.* Yes, it's basically *shut up* or get sued. Fair enough.

Section 2a.) Housing. All beta testers will receive a free apartment in the Salvos Corporation office at this address at which they must reside during the entire testing period, and during any extensions offered by Salvos Corporation, LLC. Housing is free of charge to the tenant during the testing period. That's probably part of the whole secrecy deal. Also fair enough.

I flip through the pages and slowly read the rest. Salvos needs to monitor my gaming activity for the purpose of improving the game, and I must play a minimum of twenty hours per week to remain as a beta tester and I have to offer my feedback each time I'm asked. All seems okay and I wonder why I was worrying so much. There's a bit of stuff about terminology and definitions and such.

But in short, I spot no monstrous loopholes between the lines.

One question burns. But Candi has left the room, likely to leave me to my thoughts and monitor the other players.

"Final page, then."

I flip to the last page of the contract.

Amendment 1a.) Mike Wattles shall receive a sum of $3,000 weekly, deposited into his bank account, from Salvos Corporation during the beta test period.

And below that, Anthony Anton, CEO of Salvos Corporation, already has his name stamped.

A blank line with my printed name underneath waits.

CHAPTER TWELVE

Almost feeling like a jerk with my good fortune, I get to work packing as soon as I'm back in my crap apartment. My roommates are gone but I'll leave a note and this month's rent so they have time to find another sardine.

Yeah, screw sleep.

The Wattleman is officially a closed beta tester for Salvosera.

"I can't believe this," I mutter, shoving some clothes into a garbage bag. Thankfully I don't have much and Candi even let me look at my new apartment already, which is already furnished. I can leave my leaking air mattress and crooked dresser behind. Salvos will send someone to clean out my heavy stuff for me tomorrow.

Natalie's probably sleeping at past one in the morning, so I can't drop the bomb yet. Apparently, I can tell her I'm beta testing *a* new game, but I can't give anything else other than super vague details. That's fine. I'm not going to screw this up. The amended contract let me know that's not a good idea.

And Candi also let me know it's not a good idea to tell the other testers about my pay when I meet them. Don of course has a hint, but she promised me he'd stay quiet.

"It might sow, um, discontent," she said.

I pack for the next couple of hours, forcing my eyes to stay open. Just clothes, mostly, and my old gaming platform and laptop. It's not like I have anything else for entertainment. I don't want the moldy food in the fridge and Candi let me know I'll have some at the new place to hold me over until I get paid.

Once Don texts me with my fifteen-minute warning, I kick my boxes out the apartment door and scribble my note, then leave my payment. I wonder how my roommates will take this when they get in from their night shifts. Then I stand there and take one last look at the piles of papers, pizza boxes, and crumpled fast food bags.

"Whoever comes in here next, I pity you," I say, pure excitement flooding my chest.

Don and another guy show up just after three AM, trudging up the apartment steps. Don eyes the boxes and picks one up and the other guy, a youngish dude with a ponytail, gives me a fist bump.

"It's Matt," he says. "Fellow tester."

"Hey. Nice to meet you again. Don't you guys ever sleep?"

"Once in a while." Matt puts a box under each arm as I pick up a couple myself. "I hear you're the brain. I'm the guy who does builds. Not so good at the mob traps and the auto farms."

"Is that why they picked you?" A lot of Creationist players log in so they can build cities and palaces. Some classrooms even use the game to teach kids about architecture.

"Yeah. I built a whole Mayan city in Creationist. In survival mode," Matt says. "Did a video tour on GameTube, and I got nabbed two months ago just like you did, except they took me to a different office to make the offer. I'm from the sprawling corn fields of Iowa. Now I'm here in the city."

We move the boxes down to the waiting van. Don still doesn't say much. I wonder what his specialty is.

"I saw that video!" I say, loading my two boxes. "Awesome, man." I look at Don, waiting for him to speak.

"Explorer here," he says, thumping himself on the chest. "You ever seen the GameTube series about the guy who's trying to walk to the end of the Creationist world, to the Glitch Lands?"

"Dude. You're serious." Am I staring at Comma_Volt, the GameTuber who's been walking across a Creationist world for years, trying to find where the code starts breaking down? "I would have thought you'd talk more like in your videos."

"I do that all day," Don says, shutting the back of the black SUV they've used to pick me up this time. "We're loaded up. Let's get back to HQ so we can crash before tomorrow."

I'm not ready for bed yet. "What does Candi do in Salvosera?" I ask. "She says she's done some testing, too."

Matt gets into the driver's seat. Me and Don get in as well, and I'm in the middle section, between them and my boxes. "She's out of everyone's league," Matt says as I click on my seat belt.

I breathe out my disappointment. "What do you mean?"

"She won't tell anyone what she does or why Salvos brought her on," Matt said. "Trust me, we all wonder about that. Salvos doesn't bring anyone onto the testing team unless they're capable of pushing the limits."

"Oh. Okay," I mutter.

I think of Natalie as we get rolling through Charlotte. She's a pretty good Creationist player and killer at combat and PVP, but like me, she's struggling with getting her channel off the ground. It's sheer luck Candi spotted my auto farm videos and followed me to Vox's castle map.

Matt picks up some late night drive-thru for us with a fancy-looking credit card. These two, I know, already make good money making Creationist videos. They've both got tons of subs and didn't need to ask for anything. I wonder if any of the other testers have sick family they're worried about.

Exhaustion hits me when we get back to the Salvos building. My apartment's on the third floor, and I have it all to myself. We set my boxes down in the spacious, white living room which has a leather couch and an entertainment system already set up. The kitchen is also big and not full of moldy food.

"Clean place smell," I say, inhaling and spreading my arms as I cross the threshold.

"Just try to keep it that way, okay?" Matt asks as he and Don leave, no doubt to get some sleep.

Someone's stocked the fridge with plenty of gamer fuel, AKA energy drinks, and actual food I can throw in the microwave. But I collapse on the bed in the attached bedroom and pass out.

When I wake to sunlight streaming through my huge window, I take a second to remember where I am and how lucky I just got. The sun pours through the closed blinds and I shoot out of bed, change my clothes, and call Natalie. It's Saturday and she's home at her own place, right?

"Hey, Matt."

"You'd never guess what happened." Instead of false hope, I can offer something real. A massive weight lifts off my chest. "I'm making three grand a week now, and I'm going to send you some to help out."

She's flabbergasted. Silence drags out. *"What?"*

Still in a dream state, I tell her I got drafted by Salvos to test a new game, but that I can't give it out the details. For all I know, this apartment's bugged, but I don't tell her that either. I do mention I'm working side by side with the Mayan city guy and the Glitch Lands guy. "I can't break my contract or I lose it all. I didn't want to tell you I got fired by Blob yesterday."

"Blob?"

"Landon's nickname. Officially just earned by me."

"Okay. You got hired on by Salvos Corporation. I'm jealous."

"I knew you'd be and I'm sorry. I'll put in a good word for you. I'd love to have you join us here. How you feeling?"

"Okay, mostly. My treatment starts next week and I'll have to take some time off. I'm probably going to suck at Creationist as well as at keeping my job."

"Look, Natalie. Just focus on getting better. Don't worry about that job. Yeah, they're trying to set you up, but I've got you covered if the worst happens and then you can find another job later. I won't be going out and blowing the cash because I'll be too busy playing this awesome game I can't wait for you to try. Just play Creationist. Keep making videos. You might get lucky."

"I've never been able to get anywhere. Nobody watches them."

"I had that same problem," I said. "Keep trying. People love PVP maps and those last man standing type games."

"Well, I suppose. Go have fun." Despite her disappointment, I can hear the incredible relief in Natalie's voice.

My mood's in the sky as I nuke a breakfast burrito, eat, and head down to the testing room. It's empty but the changing room is unlocked. I imagine the other testers are busy making Creationist videos and making their big money with ad revenue. They must come down here at night to play on their own time.

Well, no one will see me flailing around in the box, but how will I know how to exit the game? I never saw a menu on my two-hour trial. And since everything down here is open 24/7, I can imagine someone's monitoring my gameplay or is at least getting notifications about what I'm doing. Candi can't be expected to do that all the time.

I change into the Salvos suit and climb into the same Simulator I used the night before, not sure if it matters which one I use. The plastic pieces of the suit and the helmet tingle against my skin as the blue light hits them. Just as I wonder how the heck to log in, everything goes black as the process starts automatically.

I fall. I flail around like an idiot, waving my arms. The ground vanishes.

And then I land.

I'm lying on the floor of a now-sunlit, shallow cave and facing the ceiling. I blink as I study the smooth, but pixelated texture. My Common Leaves barrier still holds when I push myself up and look at the sparkling water of the Northern Swamp just a bit below my position. I'm back. I can no longer see the sun rising, so some time must have passed between when Candi logged me out and when I came back to Salvosera.

I equip my Flint Hatchet, which is in my six-slot hotbar. The Common Soil is gone since I used it all, but a piece of Pure Sand is still there. The hotbar must collect your most recently used items on top of accepting whatever I put in there. Cool.

Exiting the cave is uneventful. The mob drops from the Swamp Ghouls have despawned. No shocker. The pentagon sun is maybe at the ten o-clock position.

I find out I can keep my hotbar at the bottom of my vision by tapping it a couple of times, which is good.

Now I can cut down trees.

With the Flint Hatchet, breaking the Common Leaf barrier is easy and fast, though a green health bar appears for the tool, nestled inside its box. Durability. The bar's mostly still full by the time I collect all my Common Leaves and Sticks, so I should be able to cut some trees down.

My stomach rumbles as if I haven't eaten in two days.

"What?" I ask. "Seriously. I feel hunger here."

Duh. The Calories bar isn't there for nothing.

I pull up my status bars by hitting my chest. My health's stopped regenerating and is depleted by about an eighth, while my Calories bar is drained to half empty. Apparently, you don't heal unless your Calories bar is over half full.

"Thanks, Swamp Ghouls," I say. "Now I get to try the Salvosera cuisine."

I've got to find food, but more importantly, I've got to create a real shelter so I don't have a repeat of last night. I'll worry about my first mob trap after that.

I walk back uphill to the bright green, sparsely wooded area. When I tap the top of my head for the info pane, I see that this biome is just called a Scattered Forest, and the Hostility score is only thirty-three rather than seventy. I check again about fifty more steps in, and I see that the

Hostility score has dropped to twenty-five. So the score changes constantly. Interesting. Then I walk towards the cliff I saw yesterday. Back up to forty-one. So the Hostility is not the same through an entire biome. It might even be random or partially dependent on the biome.

But first things first. I approach a tree and hack at it with my hatchet. The wood cracks quickly and then breaks, dropping a log with a pentagon-shaped border. The rest of the tree stays floating. Gravity: 0. And I've taken no more damage. When I pick up the Common Wood, I see that its Resistance is 2 and it's Refinable.

I finish collecting the wood from the tree, ending up with eight Common Wood. Its Common Leaves break apart on their own, one by one, dropping sticks.

A shudder races up my spine as a sense of unease comes over me, and a second later I realize why. A sort of quiet slithering noise, almost like footsteps on grass but not quite, approaches from behind.

"Uh, oh."

I whirl, raising the Flint Hatchet.

I've been standing near a dark cave the whole time I've been massacring this tree, one almost invisible behind two other trees.

And something has just come out of it.

"What insane mind came up with this?"

The creature looks like a an orange-and-tan, bouncing coil with a square head, and a messed-up face at eye level set into a black, pained grimace. It's bouncing towards me, closing the measly ten-block gap between us.

A tiny voice in my mind speaks. *This might be bad.*

I swing my Flint Hatchet as it closes the last few feet between us and...stops.

I strike, and the creature bounces back a bit and emits a crackling sound as if it's burning inside. The sound intensifies as the coil trains its glare on me and slowly straightens up.

Before I can swing again, the creature erupts into bright orange, pixelated fire, which falls around me with a loud *whoosh*. Heat explodes over my body, intense and almost painful, as my vision flashes redder and redder. My rapidly shrinking health bar rises, and then a blob of final darkness expands across my vision.

CHAPTER THIRTEEN

Darkness rises around me. The ground is gone.

And with a *thump,* I land on my back.

"Well, crap."

I open my eyes to find myself lying on my back, at the same point where I spawned when trying out Salvosera for the first time. The blue sky stretches overhead and the hexagon sun, now almost at noon, creeps across the sky.

I just got killed by an orange coil that didn't even look happy about it. Great.

I get up and the first thing I do is feel my backpack. It's deflated and my inventory that pops in front of me is empty.

"Well, it happens to everybody," I grumble.

I've lost my items. No surprise. My hotbar's gone, too, and I know without checking that it'll be empty. The same happened in Creationist.

And then...*panic.*

My items might despawn, just like the Swamp Ghoul drops.

And I don't want to get behind and disappoint Salvos Corporation. They're paying me, after all.

I scan the Scattered Forest. Crap, where is my stuff? It should have dropped like it does in Creationist when you die.

There.

A cluster of floating leaves, minus branches or a tree trunk, slowly pops out of existence maybe fifty blocks away.

Then I spot the globs of lava on the ground. Orange, animated, and pixelated, they make seething noises as fires, a series of animated yellow and orange pixels, spring up around them and die, leaving patches of bare Common Dirt among the grass.

Heart pounding, I run towards it.

The orange coil itself is gone. It must be a mini-volcano, erupting and offing itself whenever it sees enemies. There's a nice big patch of Common Dirt where the grass has burned away. Yeah. It was standing right there, between me and that cave. The monster just destroyed itself to destroy me. What a great life it must have.

My stuff.

What happened to my stuff?

I slow and skid to a stop. I spot my Flint Hatchet on the ground along with two Common Logs, but my Sifter, Common Leaves, and Sticks all seem to be gone. Oh, and I still have that useless Pure Sand. I pick everything up in a rush as the heat from the fires and spread-out lava splotches assaults my skin, hoping I figure out the auto pickup feature soon. Yeah. I've lost half my inventory, probably to these lava splotches and the little fires.

"Well, we know what the least favorite monster is going to be," I grumble.

A nearby tree catches fire, with flames dancing over some Common Leaves. Quickly I equip my Pure Sand block, not knowing what else to do since I don't see my Flint Hatchet in its usual spot on my hotbar, but I have to stop this fire from spreading and ruining the whole area. I place the Pure Sand block over the fire, which hisses as it goes out.

And to my amazement, the Pure Sand, instead of obeying gravity, instantly morphs to a transparent pentagon with a grayish-blue border and lines through it.

"Did I just give this tree a monocle?"

It's a glass pane.

I've discovered something new.

I place the Pure Sand over the other little fires and the lava, and both have the same effect. Glass. Glorious glass. The fire and lava vanish each time and once they're gone, the temperature drops. I imagine there must be an easier way of making glass, like some kind of oven I can make.

Otherwise...

"Windows. A dangerous business since 2027."

But at least I can pick the glass up with my bare hands by "breaking" it. Even though it shows a breaking animation when I punch it, the glass drops whole.

But I'll find the uses later.

I've got to get a base going so I don't spend another night in that cave with nothing but a Hostility score of 70 to keep me company.

* * * * *

No one yanks me out of the game during that day cycle and chastises me for falling victim to a lava coil.

So I decide to build my base near the bottom of the cliff I found, the one with the greenish ore on the side that I still can't mine.

Three reasons:

1.) The cliff looks awesome and has potential for inventions.

2.) It's far away from that cave opening.

3.) It's even farther away from the Northern Swamp.

And I work quickly now that I know what to do.

I make a new Sifter and then a couple more hatchets, since one Flint Hatchet is only good for cutting down a dozen trees before it breaks. And before I know it, I have a whole collection of logs, which stack to 99 in my inventory.

And with that, I refine Common Logs into Common Planks. Literally, I just place them in my Crafting Tab and *viola!* Six Common Planks come out of each Log.

My new Sifter seems to last forever as it has no durability bar. I place it outside of the small house I'm building from the Planks, right against the outer wall.

By the evening of that day, I've got four walls set up in a rectangle, but no roof, and four small, pentagon-shaped windows from the eight Glass Panes I've collected.

"You are making progress, Wattleman," I say, ducking through the door-shaped opening I've left myself. "Basic stuff, almost done. Then you can get to the fun stuff."

The sun sets, and the big stars come out overhead and slowly drift. It gets very dark in my not-so-creative house. But I'm not much into pretty constructions. It's an area where I lack talent.

I shiver.

It's cold in a roofless house.

And I'm also still hungry.

I doubt the Ghouls and the lava coils can climb walls, but I can't be too careful. I spend the night crouching and peeking out the windows, ducking low in case monsters can see through glass, and keeping close to the wall in case something spawns on top of that cliff. I haven't built my house close enough for something to drop down on me from that height, but I'm close enough for something to see me from up there. It'll be interesting to know if any other mobs are stupid enough to off themselves. The ghouls are likely dumb enough and I already know about the lava coils.

Some mobs do spawn in the distant Scattered Forest, but nothing comes near my hiding spot, probably thanks to the solid blocks. I spot a few tall things that look like Ghouls, outlined against the stars, and a pair of those lava coils hopping around. Turns out they give off a faint orange glow at night.

The Hostility score here is 37. Not as bad as the border of that swamp. Fewer mobs seem to be spawning and the ones here don't seem to be bloodhounds, but there could be other factors keeping them away.

The hiccup-scream of an injured ghoul sounds behind me and I whirl, looking through the other window at the cliff. It's official. They're stupid enough to walk off cliffs, which I can also use to my advantage. The ghoul stands there, advancing towards the house from maybe twenty blocks away, and I guess that it saw me from above and dropped down after me.

My stomach rumbles and my status bars rise into my vision.

Can Putrid Flesh be turned into fertilizer? That's the only use I can think of for it, other than feeding tamed animals like Goats.

I've got to try it, because now my Calories bar is down by two-thirds.

I hack away two Common Planks to make a doorway and charge outside at the injured ghoul. As the sun slowly rises, I can see that this one is brown instead of green-blue—a Common Ghoul, probably—and it dies with one swing of my Hatchet, dropping its Putrid Flesh. A second ghoul takes a suicide dive off the cliff, following the first, and I dispatch that one, also brown, and pick up its drops.

Something flutters above me and in the distance.

I turn to face it.

A gigantic moth, black against the pink morning sky, flutters aimlessly above the trees in the distance. Instinct takes over and I run back through the makeshift doorway of my house. I've got to get some farming going, yes, but first I'm going to need a roof.

CHAPTER FOURTEEN

I figure out how to make roof panels in my Crafting Tab. Common Roof Panels are pretty much flat planks and I can make six by putting three Common Planks in a diagonal formation. Turns out they make a good angled roof but after the incident with that orange coil thing, I know they're in danger of burning. Still, it's better than nothing.

"And now, the Mike Wattles House of Mediocrity," I say, spreading my arms before my creation.

Well, I do have Common Logs as outer corner trim so it's not completely the same color, but other than that? Bleh. I will not impress anyone with my matching Common Plank roof on top of the plain Common Plank rectangle. But that's not what I'm here for, I remind myself.

But at least, over the next couple of in-game day cycles, I learn how to make other tools through the art of experimentation. Flint Chisel? I get that by combining a stick and a Flint Shard, one above the other, without Plant Twine. Flint Backhoe? Two Common Sticks, a Plant Twine, and one Flint Shard in the general shape of one. Flint Shovel? Two Common Sticks in a vertical formation, then two Plant Twine on the top row and a Flint Shard between them. That last one takes me a while to figure out as it's not as intuitive.

"Now this has promise." I stand in my house and raise my new Flint Hammer as the sun rises on yet another day. "This just might break stone or put an even bigger dent in that lava coil's face."

My stomach rumbles again, more intense than ever, but when I pull up my status bars I see that Calories has slowed its downward march. I've got a bit more than a quarter remaining. But my health hasn't recovered past that final one-eighth, either. The slowdown is a strange mechanic but I'm glad I won't have to worry about food constantly.

But *constantly* is the thing.

I still need to worry.

And the time for that is now. Something will happen if my Calories bar drops too low.

I exit the house, using the actual Common Door I made in my Crafting Tab (six Common Planks in two columns of three) which opens with a charming *click* sound. The pink sky is rapidly turning to blue. I must be on Day Five or so by now. I eye the ore in the cliff, but decide to go to the swamp first to see if those stupid ghoul things have left any drops for me to scavenge.

Because overnight, I figured out how to make a Common Trapdoor, a Fence Post, and a Compost Bin just from trying different combos of Common Planks. And if there's anything I can compost, it's Putrid Flesh. I've figured out that refinable items can either be refined in my Crafting Tab, or on some placeable utility block like the Sifter.

If Putrid Flesh passes the Yuck Test, have I got an idea for a mob trap.

The land slopes downward to the Northern Swamp and I spot a few bones and pieces of that disgusting flesh on the ground, but no living Swamp Ghouls. The only ones spawning now must be underground, and so far I've only seen them spawn in water, in the dark. I pick up the drops and slowly turn.

"So, The House of Mediocrity is about a hundred blocks from here," I mutter. "I was there all night, which means mobs can spawn at least a hundred blocks away from me. And there's a small pond just inside the Northern Swamp biome."

Aha.

Lightbulb moment.

I'm about to talk about the next part of my plan when a dark, fluttering form from above makes my heart stop.

I look up, glimpsing blocky, yet pointed green wings just ten feet above my head. A moth with a body the size of me descends, blowing wind against my face, and each time it spreads its green wings, I see another grimace in its dark spots.

"I hope you're passive." I haven't checked the area for leftover night mobs well enough.

An ear-splitting screech fills the air.

Nope.

I duck under one of the Common Trees as the monster emits a sound worthy of an alarm clock and shoots a pixelated ball of green goo at me. But it lands with a hiss on some leaves, spreading out despite hanging over air and dripping particles onto the ground. The acid stuff only lasts a few seconds and misses me by inches, but the leaf block it struck has just vanished, dropping nothing.

Great. A ranged mob. And at some point I switched my tool to...my shovel. But my hotbar's up and I tap my Flint Hammer with my free hand. A new weight makes me drop my right hand as the shovel turns into the hammer.

"Come at me!"

And the moth lowers.

It can't fit under the tree with me or touch the ground. Instead, the monster flutters there, waiting, exposing its bottom half.

"Who has their pants down now?" Gripping the Hammer with both hands, I swing. *Thunk.* While slow, the Hammer has great knockback. The moth flashes red and flies back several feet with an even louder than normal screech.

And it stays there, hovering in place, waiting for me to emerge.

It's a lot less stupid than the ghouls.

And now if I run, it'll let me know what dissolving in acid feels like.

"Think, Mike," I mutter, wishing I'd done more combat. But I stay under the tree, which I name Camp Coward. The moth remains. We're having an Old West standoff and one of us needs to march forward.

"Don't run." Shaking, I emerge from under the tree, clearing my vision of leaves and facing the monster head-on, hoping to draw it back to me. Its eyes are black pentagons. Its body, segmented and brown. Somewhere, a Duck quacks.

Another ball of green crap sails at me without warning.

And before I can back under the tree, it strikes.

Heat flares and red flashes. It rivals what I felt with the fire. I step back, out of a floating block of green stuff, as everything flashes red and I keep taking damage. The tree. Camp Coward. I belong there. My health bar drops lower and lower, past half, as I take shelter. Then it stops and the heat vanishes.

My Health and Calories are both now a quarter full.

No. It's even worse. My Calories bar drops to just below that, but I don't heal. So taking damage depletes it. My knees start to shake and my arms feel like rubber.

And a cartoon icon of a hand with shaking, squiggly lines around it appears in the upper right corner of my vision, and stays there. A status effect, probably Weakness or something, thanks to being so hungry or low on health.

I lift the hammer as the moth finally draws close to my tree again. It's gained ten pounds or maybe that's just the Weakness.

"Think, Mike."

If I take another hit, I'm dead.

Without a thought, I charge forward and swing with my hammer again, taking advantage of that pause between slimeballs. I grunt with the effort, but I hit the moth and this time, the creature falls to the side, reddening and exploding into dust particles.

I breathe out and curse.

"This heavy Flint Hammer just proved itself." I try to calm down since my heart is racing. Two hits. It's heavy and the knockback is a disadvantage with ranged mobs, but it deals a lot of damage. Then I straighten and check its tooltip in my inventory.

Flint Hammer
Strength: 2
Attack: 7 (10 Critical)
Speed: -3
Health: 150/150
Calories: -5

Well, that explains at least part of the Calorie drop. And I might have scored a critical hit by charging with this weapon or hitting the moth in the right place.

I close my inventory, wondering what to do next. Two drops lay on the ground: a green, rectangular plate looking thing and what looks like a spool of silk. I take them both. A Dreadmoth Plate. Refinable. And just plain Silk. Not refinable. I imagine both are good for making armor, given their names.

Which I am going to need, right along with food, because the lack of both are becoming an issue.

Somewhere in the nearby swamp, a Duck quacks and floats on top of the gross water. I swim out, kill it with my Hammer, and pick up the Raw Duck now floating on top of the water. "Wow, I am glad Salvos didn't make drops sink." I'm hungry, but not that hungry. And the Northern Swamp is complete with muck that I can feel under my boots.

Shivering, I wade back out of the water. I'm close to the cave where I spent my first night, as well as the spot where I dug out some of the Damp Soil. I'll need fuel to cook the Raw Duck and that stuff down there looks promising, almost like buried charcoal. This game's too realistic for me to eat it as is. And yes, the dark stuff still waits where I exposed it, and while I'm there, I find I can dig up some clods of it with my shovel.

Clump of Peat
Resistance: 2
Speed: −1
Fall Damage: −1
Gravity: 0
Refinable: 1
Fuel: 1

"Okay, Mike. Don't panic. You have food and gas. Wow, that didn't sound right," I mutter, leaving the small mine I've started. It's full of that Peat stuff, so full that it might run under the whole Northern Swamp. I've gathered a few dozen pieces of the stuff, and it seems each block of Peat drops four to five clods.

My arms quiver, probably thanks to that Weakness debuff I've got. And my Calories bar has dropped a bit more. Using tools seems to slowly make me hungry.

"Time to go back to base." The pentagon sun sinks towards the horizon and vanishes behind the giant cliff.

And now I get to mine stone which will probably require the Hammer.

I still can't break that green ore in the cliff, but the rest of the stone breaks into pentagon-shaped chunks of Common Stone. As the sun sets, I go inside and try to make an oven by drawing a sort of box in my Crafting Tab with them. Then I try multiple other shapes in my grid. A U. A sideways U. An upside down U. Then two rows of three.

No go.

"What gives?"

My stomach rumbles and cramps. It seems like the logical next step to make a stone oven, unless I need some sort of glue to keep the stone together. So far, Salvosera has mostly been good and intuitive if you use your brain, but I've spotted some inconsistencies. Well, it *is* a beta test.

But frustration builds as I try a few more patterns and get nothing except for some Common Stone Slabs and a

Common Stone Walkway. Then I make some Slabs and try those in the shape of a box. Still nothing.

"Great. I'm stuck." And I'm still shaking, feeling as if I've just recovered from the flu.

And just as I utter those words, I feel the pull of the logout sequence.

"No," I yell, wanting to solve this, and now.

I fall through the dark as I utter a few choice words, and then I find myself back in the glass box with the blue light shining down on me. Stunned, I whirl on the roller balls and face Candi, now dressed in her own Salvos suit minus the helmet. She's opening the door to my Simulator.

And in that suit, she's hot. It's an exercise of pure will not to stare.

"Mike," she says. "Having trouble?" She keeps her voice low as if she doesn't want anyone else to hear even though I think Don is walking along through his own Simulator, beside mine, and lost in his own world.

I hate to admit it. "Maybe. Some things in this game I've figured out, and others not so much."

"Yes. That's why it's a beta," Candi says. Then she leans in and whispers with the most serious look in her green eyes. "They're watching you, Mike. We might have made a mistake, and they're looking for the first chance to get rid of you."

And with that, she closes my door, forces a smile, and walks away.

CHAPTER FIFTEEN

Of course I'm not going to stand there while she walks away, carrying the answers I need. Watching me? A mistake? What mistake? I signed the contract and read all the terms, fair and square. And Candi told me that Salvos needs an inventor.

Candi continues into the changing room and closes the door behind her. Her laptop sits on a small table beside the door. I piece together the scenario. Candi saw me struggling so she wasn't in the game during the time. She must have been about to go into the game herself when she did one last check on me.

And now apparently, not learning how to cook could ruin everything.

I wait for Candi to get changed. Don continues his hike, oblivious that I'm right there.

I get out and wait. She emerges from the changing room a moment later, dressed in her professional suit that still adds curves in all the right places. Her green eyes invite me to say something while also warning me to be cautious. Then she flicks her gaze to the ceiling.

And for the first time, I notice the round, black globes that hide cameras.

"Thanks for checking up on me. How long was I in there?" I force a stupid, cringe-worthy smile.

She crosses her arm and smiles. "Eight hours."

"Eight *hours?*" My jaw falls open. *Good job, Mike.*

"We cut people off after that amount of time," Candi says, acting as if she hasn't just told me that I'm one step away from a cliff. "Otherwise, we'll be breaking out adult diapers and that is *not* in my job description."

"You'd need to demand hazard pay."

Candi laughs. "Well, we have the minibar. Salvosera has no way to warn players they're spending too long in the game yet. The devs really need to work on that or they're going to deal with damage control. I've been watching your gameplay for the past few hours, off an on. You were getting involved. I was about to log into my own world, but I've already got in my twenty hours for the week, so I figured taking a break tonight might be a good idea."

"Yeah. Maybe." Then I shake my head as I realize what she's saying. We can talk away from the hidden cams. "Um, Candi? Were you thinking dinner tonight? I'm starving, in Salvosera *and* in real life."

Silence falls.

We stare at each other.

I've just asked Candi out to dinner. I might not have said *date,* but the meaning is there. She's hot. Out of my league, as Matt and Don warned me. There's no way—

"Sure. I'm starving myself."

—she'll say yes.

She's just said yes.

But before I can gauge the full situation, she whips out her phone. "How about Pizoli's?"

* * * * *

I've got no car so have to rely on one of the Salvos Corporation's Mercedes to get there. At least Candi and Don are authorized to use one of the four vehicles in the underground garage. She drives and we finally arrive at the restaurant, a fancy Italian place I've never dined at before.

Just me and her.

Out of your league, man.

"I haven't been paid yet," I say, eyeing the fancy string lights and the elegant tables. "I don't think I can buy us—"

"Don't worry about it. I have this." She flashes me a credit card in Anthony Anton's name and an evil grin at the same time. "The big cheese knows the testers need to get out once in a while."

Candi has the CEO's credit card? Who is she, his long lost daughter? It's clear that we testers aren't on even ground, then. I haven't figured out this new world yet and I have to start now.

Candi gets us seated at a small table in the far corner of the room. "How did you get that?" I ask, feeling small.

She thumbs through her phone. The chances of this being a date? Currently five out of ten. "I've been with the testers for a few months. You get perks once you prove yourself." Her tone warns me not to press further.

Chances of this being a date: now four out of ten, and it'll plunge to one or two if I keep asking prying questions. Maybe Candi signed a contract stopping her from talking about her role here. I hold back a sigh. Maybe she brought me here only to discuss how screwed I am if I don't figure out all of Salvosera's game mechanics by tomorrow. At least she gave me the clear signal on that. "So, I take it corporate is watching us all when we play."

"Yes. I get access to the feeds, though they're not that interested in my opinion of the other players. They're all business types. Anthony Anton. Nate Hicks, the co-founder. And Robert Gratt, Andy's son-in law. I talked to them on the phone earlier. They expect more out of you, Mike." Candi leans forward, lowering her voice to a whisper. She taps her closed phone as she speaks as if it's very important. "I pitched you, but I agree you need time to figure out Project 93." Her gaze flicks to the surrounding diners. "The thing is, and I didn't know this, but Miriam was not supposed to alter your contract."

I swallow as the chatter of the other diners seems to go up in volume. It fills my head and I get what she's saying.

"Corporate doesn't like that they're paying me now," I hiss.

Candi nods. "Miriam is on probation. You didn't hear this from me." She sits back and turns her gaze down to her menu. Almost as if she's ashamed to face me.

Corporate never wanted to pay me.

That's the mistake.

But why is it a big deal? Anton's a millionaire. An eccentric recluse, but a millionaire. And I signed the contract. They can't go back now. But with the phone still sitting on the table, possibly monitoring our conversations if we're loud enough, I don't dare ask.

I grab the edge of the fancy menu and pinch it between my fingers. I've got to change the subject. She's made it clear that I need to wow Salvos and all I can do is move to the next step. "I think I'm coming along in the game. Back in Creationist, I took forever to learn everything. I took my time." Candi *had* pitched me, that was for sure. I just hoped she hadn't made me sound like a charity case, trying to get dough for my sister.

She swallows. "I explained that as well. You need time. We all do. But time is of the essence."

I sit there as a waiter walks up and asks what we want to drink. Absently I order some root beer. Once he leaves, I say, "I understand. I need to step up my game." I can do that, but I might need some hints. Salvos wants that guy who made that auto mummy farm. A thousand drops per hour, max efficiency.

"Beta testing is supposed to go into a new phase soon. I don't have all the details yet, so stay tuned." Candi takes her drink from the waiter, a glass of water. "Just don't cause any stinks."

She means telling the other testers I'm getting paid. "I won't. You've got total cooperation out of me." A heavy feeling settles into my chest.

Chances this is a date: currently two out of ten. Candi doesn't seem mad but she's not giving me any lovey-dovey vibes either. She's here as a friend, giving me advice.

My root beer sucks and tastes watery. Despite the disappointment, I need more answers.

Candi nods. "You get how it works."

"I'm from a call center. Everston Hosting."

She already knows that, though. "By the way, you did great against that Dreadmoth. And everyone dies to a Lavaworm early in the game. Consider it a rite of passage. Just don't forget your special obligations."

"My what?" I don't remember reading that in my contract, but it had been late at night. "Special obligations?"

Candi looks at me, all confused. "Yeah. Where you need to display your special skills?"

"I swear I never read that." Did I miss a page? A hollow feeling fills my chest.

"You might want to look at your contract again. I had Liz slide your copy under your door. Oh, she's another player," Candi said.

"I will. But it just seems weird. All games have wikis. Why don't we have one we can share just amongst ourselves? I used the wiki for Creationist all the time when figuring out my builds. Salvos is making this very hard."

"It's all new ground and they don't want any information online for competitors or hackers to find," Candi said, and not without regret. "I think you just need a bit more time. You're working on the farming, which should turn out to be a very good source of resources, and you're on your way to some mob traps."

I drop my shoulders, glad she seems confident. "Hey, how the heck do you make an oven or campfire, by the way?"

The waiter returns for our food orders. We let him know what we want but Candi flashes me a frown as soon as he's gone.

"Players aren't supposed to exchange advice," she says. "We can talk a bit, but pure advice is against the rules. We're all supposed to mold Salvosera in our own unique way." Candi fixes me in an intense stare and I know she's trying to tell me something. Each word might be important. "That's why they keep us all in the dark. Where the monsters are, so to say."

"That makes sense. Maybe I need to take a break when I'm getting frustrated. Think over what I'm doing." Candi might not be interested in me in that way, but she's given me some help and some possible clues. She's still on my side.

And I'm going to sleep on and mull over every single one of her words.

Natalie's life might depend on it.

CHAPTER SIXTEEN

I crash in my new apartment that night, landing on my bed and going over Candi's words. Shoving aside the disappointment that our dinner hadn't been a date, I eye the brown envelope Liz slid under my door that contains my copy of the contract. I should go over it again, but I need to deal with a couple of things first. One, I've got to fill in Natalie. Two, I need to figure out Candi's clues.

We're all supposed to *mold* Salvosera. The monsters are in the *dark.* I've figured out that darkness spawns them already but Candi's provided confirmation that it might be usable for mob traps. I either have to find it or create it. The molding part just might have to do with making my first oven which I'm leaning towards instead of a campfire. But what about the farming? I'll have to explore that once I log back in tomorrow.

There's something there beyond what I've suspected, then.

I call Natalie from my position on the bed. "How's it going?"

"Had my first treatment today. I feel like crap." Her voice is strained and tired. "Well, I've got two sick days left."

"Don't worry. I get paid this Friday. Direct deposit, and then I'm sending most of it to you. Even if you lose your insurance, three grand per week adds up to well, a lot of cash."

"It does. Mike, you're a literal lifesaver. And I should be fine so long as I get this treatment. I've got the more chronic form of leukemia."

"But you don't need medical bills to ruin your life."

She forces a laugh. "Well, some people say dying is easier than medical bills."

I gulp. "Sometimes, it is. I've heard horror stories. And I still need to put in a word for you. See if Salvos needs a PVP person. I guess beta is supposed to go into a new phase soon and they want a certain lineup of players." So far, I've met a few of them, but not everyone. I'm guessing there are a half dozen players in this mostly empty apartment complex.

"Well, I might not be up for it for a bit. So take your time. I've got a Last Man Standing tournament in half an hour. Gotta go."

"Send me the link and I'll watch." I smile, glad Natalie is still able to play.

I spend the rest of the night on my bed, watching the GameTube stream that Natalie's set up. I'm one of fifteen viewers. She's plays another one of Vox's awesome adventure maps, The Barrens, which is full of ruins that a dozen players raid for weapons and scarce resources. For the first hour, Natalie dodges other players scattered around the map, loots ruins for resources, and skirts death by Phantoms several times. Once the horn sounds at the end of that hour, she's teleported to the center of the map with the eight other players who are still alive, and I tense as I watch her dodge and shoot her Crossbow, taking down three people in a row.

Natalie earns a few small donations and a new subscriber. Her side feed briefly fills with praise and emojis as she takes out the second-to-last opponent using an enchanted sword she found in a Loot Crate. But then the last player slays her from behind, leaving her in second place. Not bad.

Only rarely does she place less than third.

I give her a thumbs-up in the comments section, a donation of fifteen dollars (all I can manage at the moment) and go to bed, feeling hopeful for her.

But I'm also sad to notice that neither of her new subscribers are *CandiofSummer* or *AASalvosCorp*.

* * * * *

Ding dong. I have my very first Salvosera mob trap.

And better yet, it's only taken me a few more in-game days to figure out.

The mob farm is even uglier than the House of Mediocrity and not super efficient, but for now, it works. My stomach rumbles as I look at the square, Damp Soil mini-skyscraper. It's dark inside but open at the front, but into a roofless chute made of more Damp Soil and filled with Common Leaves.

"And behold," I say, "the Mike Wattles Swamp Ghoul Factory Farm."

Since I've determined that I hate Swamp Ghouls (turns out they're tougher than Common Ghouls), they're my first target.

And I've also discovered a handful of tips that I might add to a wiki in the future.

1.) Swamp Ghouls have twice the health of Common Ghouls, but also twice the drops, making them more valuable than the wimpy type. And yes, they do only spawn in swamp water.

2.) Monsters try to spawn all the time, judging from the sounds I hear underground. They're always limited to dark places, and some die in the sun.

3.) Swamp Ghouls can spawn on the surface during the daytime so long as there's darkness over a body of swamp water. And yes, I built this eyesore over a pond of swamp water.

4.) Higher Hostility levels make mobs spawn like crazy. Right here, it's 70. Which is good.

5.) Swamp Ghouls are dumb enough to push through Common Leaves to get to me, even if they're, say, ten meters thick.

6.) Mobs won't spawn less than twenty meters away from me, meaning I have to stand twenty-one blocks from my Factory Farm for it to start cranking out the livestock.

"And during the day, I kill three Swamp Ghouls a minute just by standing here," I say, satisfied, from my spot at the end of the Slaughter Chute. "And *that* won't get annoying."

The constant tune of Ghouls taking sun damage assaults my ears, but none make it to me before dying. All I have to do is stand there and wait. One by one, the monsters march out into the sunny arms of death.

Before I *really* figured out my first trap, I had just one tiny problem: the Bones and the Putrid Flesh I need for compost would end up sitting deep within the leaves, jittering around and not glitching out at me like I'd hoped. That meant I had the choice between cutting the leaves away and replacing them each time I wanted my drops, or just accepting defeat.

I needed a filter.

So the in-game night before last, I went to the House of Mediocrity to think it over.

Glass Panes.

They're flat, easily placeable...and can be walked on like solid blocks. And no matter what I tried, they always placed vertically.

I now had a way to separate items from dying monsters.

The downside? Since I don't yet have an oven, I had to anger and explode a couple of Lavaworms and then attack the results with Pure Sand, but it worked.

Once I had my resources, I dug a three-meter deep trench under all the leaves and replaced the Ghouls' walking surface with Glass Panes.

And that brings me to my last point:

7.) Glass Panes are great for mob traps and act as item filters. They even float when the dirt is dug out from under them.

I stand back from the Slaughter Chute and watch as two Swamp Ghouls trudge towards me, turning red and taking damage. They fall over, deep in the leaves, and from this angle I see their drops fall through the Glass Panes and into the trench. I climb down my Common Plank Stairs and collect them, realizing that I've now got sixty Putrid Flesh and sixty-three Bones.

This had better get me farming.

Because my stomach has been rumbling for the past several in-game days and my limbs are still shaking from what turned out to be Fatigue. And my health is still crap. The only thing that's saved my life so far is the fact that Lavaworms are slow to burst into fire and lava, and they stay still while doing so, giving me time to dodge. The risk is having them sneak up behind you. Or having them burst close to your wooden house.

Cursing the fact that I have no automatic way to collect drops yet, I walk back to the House of Mediocrity in the setting sun. It's visible between all the Common Trees, though my hastily-planted Mike Wattles Tree Farm blocks part of the view. Two rows of ten trees, planted from the somewhat-rare Common Tree Sprouts that drop from broken leaves, have already grown there.

I've figured out what Candi meant by the darkness. It's the key to mob traps. I know I can probably do better once I explore and conquer some caves, much better, but I'm in no shape to do that right now.

First, my health is still terrible and these mobs are tough.

Second, I need to eat.

Third, I haven't figured out how to light the Peat Torches I've managed to make.

My knees shake as I enter what I call my yard. I've managed to make a Flint Backhoe and till some land next to my house, and was shocked to have a few Barley Seeds pop out of the grass when I did, which I planted. The crops are slowly growing, appearing as green dots in the tilled land, but at this rate I won't be eating for the next week. Clearly compost is something I need, so I place all my Putrid Flesh in the Compost Bin and enter my house.

There's nothing I can do but wait on this front, so I turn my thoughts to my next issue: how the heck do I get an oven?

CHAPTER SEVENTEEN

Okay, Candi. I get the darkness. I get the farming. Sort of.

"What was that about players molding their experience?" I mutter, keeping my voice low in case Salvos is listening.

I pace around the empty house and past a Storage Crate (made by filling a Crafting Grid with Common Planks.)

"Molding. Experience. Sounds like an art class," I grumble. Then I stop, facing my front door. "Wait."

Does clay exist in Salvosera? Clay, or mud, or something?

Well, if mud existed that swamp would have had a massive inventory. Damp Soil's the closest and I've already caused enough ugly with that.

Candi wouldn't have told me that in such a serious tone if there wasn't something important behind it. And clay seems like a material that could make a primitive, first tier oven. Maybe everything here happens in tiers, just like with the tools and the resistance scores, and I need to make a clay oven before I can make a stone one.

I open the Storage Crate I've made by tapping it and opening its inventory box which looks like mine, but with a lighter wood background. I eye my Unlit Peat Torches. My Common Soil. Some Pure Sand. The Wooden Pail I made while waiting out last night. Still a noob inventory. One thing is clear: I've got to get out of here and explore when the sun comes up. Until then, I'll think about my farming issue.

I remove my Wooden Pail by tapping (three Common Planks in a V formation with a single Plant Twine on the inside) and it looks almost useless due to the holes between the boards, which are obvious even as a flat sprite.

I have yet to add water to my farmland, but the pond where I originally got the Rocky Sand is close, so I dart out into the dusk and scoop up some water before running back into the house.

It's heavy.

I feel like I'm eighty years old as I drag it back to my garden, waddling side to side.

"Well, TheWattleman's name finally checks out," I grunt.

A flash of orange to my side makes me change course to the house instead, and I lug the pail, now heavy with water, to the storage crate. A look outside confirms a Lavaworm is bouncing towards the house, and it stops at the window, staring at me with that horrible grimace.

"You know, that's rude," I say. "I don't want your pamphlets."

At least I've learned that Lavaworms won't start their death sequence unless there's nothing between my eye level and the monster. So it stands there, stares some more, and bounces off into the night.

"Stay gone," I mutter as my stomach rumbles again. So far I've been lucky, but I could stumble into a Hostility 80 area when I explore whatever is on the other side of that cliff. And my health has not recovered past that low mark. My hunger's slowly dipping below that one-quarter point.

If I don't eat, I'll die soon. Or worse, Fatigue is tiered and I'll find out what Fatigue II feels like.

The sun finally rises, and I select my Pail and lug it outside. Then I try to drop it to the ground, which only succeeds in water spilling all over my feet.

"Great. I get to do that again."

I use my Flint Shovel to dig out a hole beside the five pieces of farmland I've tilled and planted. One of the barley plants has grown a tiny bit, and as I watch, the one beside it does the same. "Fantastic. They'll be done in maybe six days instead of seven."

I fill the Pail again. Pouring the water into the hole beside the farmland works. Buckets apparently hold one square meter's worth of water, and the pixelated blue liquid fills the hole without spreading out. Then I watch as the farmland darkens and two of the barley plants instantly morph to their next growth phase. I've probably halved the time they'll take to grow.

Then an earthy, but rotten smell hits me. "Mike, you can't blame yourself, because you haven't even eaten," I mutter. Then I turn. "Oh. I guess that worked."

A brownish material with small white spots now fills it. As I draw closer, I catch the stench it's giving off, like frog belches crossed with cow indigestion.

"Salvos," I lament. "Why did you have to add this to the game? Please let me be able to mine this with my shovel. I am praying to you, Anthony Anton."

Somewhere, he's laughing. He and Vox should get together for a drink.

I stick my Flint Shovel in, dig, and instantly break a polygon of it off the top. The level in the bin drops. I dig out seven more. So filling the bin with like 64 Putrid Flesh gets me eight pieces of Compost. That's a lot of dead Swamp Ghouls.

It had better be good.

I try to drop the Compost on the farmland, but no go. Maybe I have to craft top-tier, awesome dirt with it, so I go back inside, pull a stack of Common Soil out of the Storage Crate, and put them together, side by side, in my Crafting Tab.

"Bingo."

One Compost and one Common Soil gets me two pieces of Fertile Soil, a black soil that doesn't look disgusting.

And better yet, it doesn't smell disgusting, either.

Once I have sixteen Fertile Soil, I run back outside and replace my farm. No new seeds pop up from it, so I till a few more chunks of grass and watch some pop out. Soon I'll be able to compare the types of farmland and the growth rates, but I'll do science later.

I just need food.

And at the rate the seeds are growing now, I might have it by nightfall.

But I also don't want to waste daylight. I eye the farmland that forms four rows between me and my house, glad I've cracked that nut. I'll think of an auto farm later. Putting my Wooden Pail back in my inventory, I set out to take what I hope is a short walk around the massive cliff that separates me from whatever is on the other side.

* * * * *

It's a *long* walk through more Scattered Forest, and when I finally round the cliff ten thousand years later, the world opens.

The grass here is slightly more yellow than in the biome I just left. Only a few trees stand here and there, the same common type that's surrounded me for almost my entire experience. The rest is grass and gentle hills. It's probably a builder's dream, an area where Don would build a city. And I can see for some distance. A few Ducks stand around scattered ponds and there are even a few open caves on the surface, leading down into pure darkness.

"On task, Mike," I tell myself, pulling up my hotbar with my tools. "Daylight's running out." I tap the top of my head to check the Hostility of this place.

Twenty-two. And this is a Flatlands biome, temperature of sixty. And I still have the Fatigue status effect, which has appeared under all the other stats.

"Not bad." With luck I'll have a peaceful area if I have to hunker down for the night.

If clay is anywhere, it's near water or under the dirt. Shovel ready, I approach the Ducks, who keep jumping up and down like morons between swimming in the ponds. A few Goats spawn in the distance, too, as well as a few brown hogs. Yeah. Peaceful area, unless those hogs or boars are defensive.

Pure Sand lines the ponds here, and I spot a few blocks of it, on the bottom of the closest pond, that are a rusty orange color instead of golden.

Clay?

I dig it up from the edge of the pond and watch the polygon drop as several messy globs chunks of the material. The sprites look like dripping orbs. At least the water here is warm when I get in and tap each piece.

Clay. It's clay. "I just figured out Candi's clues, because I'm really smart," I sing.

And it's refinable, probably into bricks.

The light level begins to lower, and I know night's about to come.

"Out of the hot tub," I say, pulling myself back onto flat ground. Water particles dance as I dry off in seconds.

Running back home will be suicide. So I run to the cliff, the far side, and dig myself a hole in the stone with my Flint Hammer. Once I've got a rectangular hiding spot, I block it off with one Common Dirt, leaving myself a window.

My Calories bar drops a bit more, thanks to my use of the Hammer.

I just might have to eat that Raw Duck. Shudder.

The night's quiet, and I only see two regular Ghouls and a single Lavaworm in the distance. The Lavaworm seems to come from not a cave, but from an area of light some distance away. The monsters despawn by the time the sun rises, and I emerge from my hidey-hole and get to work figuring out this clay business.

I don't waste energy talking. I can't refine the Clay Globs in my Crafting Tab, so maybe I need a brick mold. After cutting down a tree and killing a few more Ducks (they're annoying and I don't miss them) I figure out I can make a Brick Mold with Common Wood Slabs (eight arranged in a square.) By the end of the day, I have a row of them resting in the sun which I figure will only help speed up the drying process. And I can place Clay Globs in them the same way I place blocks and items on the Sifter.

I hide again during the next night, and when I emerge the following morning, I find that all the bricks I've made have hardened and turned dark. A brick color, actually.

I collect them by tapping, determined to finally cook all this Raw Duck I've collected.

And then I remember that I've left my Peat at home.

"Good job, Mike," I say. "You can't afford another trip. Soon Candi's going to pull you out of the game and give you another warning." Would that be a bad thing? I must be running out of time before she tosses me an adult diaper.

I need a fuel, and fast.

Wait.

What was that glow I saw in the distance, at night?

"Worth a check." With bricks in my inventory, I walk in that direction, unable to run more than a few paces at a time thanks to the Fatigue. The ground indents downward near where I saw the glow, and I stop, facing an orange, animated pond of not water, but lava. It seethes and heat belches from the volcanic pit.

My heart soars.

If that's not fuel, nothing is.

I pull up my inventory. And see my Wooden Pail.

Nope. Worst Idea Ever. Even a total noob should know better. Using any pail would be risky in real life, but there has to be some way to collect lava. So I rush back to my temporary hole-in-the-wall base and take my Dried Clay Bricks, arranging them in a V. Nothing. Then I take a few extra Clay Globs and do the same.

And a bucket appears in the output. No Plant Twine needed. Clay isn't great, but a better bet than wood, so I take the Damp Clay Bucket and place it outside to dry. A bit of waiting later, I have a Dried Clay Bucket.

As the sun sets, I run back out to the lava.

"If this doesn't work," I said, "I don't know what to do."

Then I remember my experience with lugging the water, and dread wells into my chest.

Leaning down, I hold out the bucket and highlight a pentagon-shaped block of lava. I pick up the lava by shoving the Bucket at it, and it fills as heat threatens to boil my arms off. The pail is hot to touch, but not unbearable, and I trudge back to my hole with my bucketful of death.

Lava is *heavy*.

Especially with Fatigue. I walk at Landon's pace as full night falls, glad that few mobs spawn here. My arms quiver. *Do not drop this. Do not drop this.* "Do not drop this."

I get back inside and gently set down the bucket with a sigh of relief. It lights my hidey-hole a bit and fills it with heat. A seething sound fills the air and sends a shudder down my spine.

This is risky.

I could die out here, experimenting with this stuff. And then I'll have to come all the way back. Once the sun rises, I'm taking all of this home. And *then* I'll do something stupid that gets me killed.

* * * * *

Luckily no one logs me out of the game, though I don't know how much time has passed in real life. I manage to make a Clay Oven (eight Dried Clay Bricks in a square formation) before the sun comes up, which breaks with the use of my hammer and drops as an item. And when the sun comes up, I have the joy of picking up that Clay Lava Pail and trudging around the cliff with it.

"This had better just be the Fatigue making this so hard." I eye my house a long walk later, as the pentagon sun sinks to the horizon. I am so sick of hugging this bucket of lava and having sweat drip into my eyes that if Salvos has this as a constant feature and not just a Fatigue punishment, I'm going to kill them myself. At last, I gently put it down next to my beautiful rows of fully-grown, golden barley crops. As expected, all of those planted in the Fertile Soil are fully grown.

"At least one thing is going right," I say. "Now, I'm ready for some food."

I fish my Clay Oven and my five Raw Duck out of my inventory and into my hotbar. I'm drooling. After placing the Oven on the ground, which looks like a box made of bricks with two dark rectangles for slots, I tap it, bringing up a stone-rimmed box with a slot for fuel, a slot for whatever's being cooked, and an output slot. I can slide the Raw Duck from my inventory into it just fine, but I still can't put the lava in my inventory to begin with, and it turns out I have to exit the Oven's GUI and pick up the bucket of lava (again) and shove my bucket at the bottom, dark rectangle of the Oven, which highlights as I aim at it.

To say this is a butt clench moment is an understatement.

Weight lifts off my arms as all the lava in the bucket vanishes.

And the Clay Oven bursts to life, with an orange glow emanating from the lower rectangle. The sounds of sizzling and the smells of meat cooking fill the air, and my stomach roars. I tap the Oven again and find two pieces of Raw Duck already done and in the output, which I tap to pull out.

Food.

At long last.

And the Cooked Duck is glistening, glorious, and tastes just like the real thing.

I devour both pieces, mouth watering, as my Calories bar rapidly fills. My Health bar ticks upward, too, and the Shaking Hand of Fatigue icon vanishes. Strength flows into my limbs as both bars climb to almost full.

I feel great.

Until a hiss and a seething sound builds from the Clay Oven.

"Um." I back away from it, sensing that despite my caution, I've just committed one of the Seven Deadly Sins of Salvosera.

The Clay Oven vanishes with another hiss, dropping as an item along with three finished Cooked Duck. And in its place sits an expanding blob of lava, which promptly rolls downhill and towards my wooden house.

CHAPTER EIGHTEEN

The Second Deadly Sin of Salvosera. Thou shall not use lava in a Clay Oven.

Melted. Gone. I watch as my Cooked Duck and the Clay Oven drops float on top of the lava for a bit before bursting into flames and vanishing with another hiss. The lava continues to spread downhill as panic seizes me and I whirl, looking for any water source. It's already halfway to my farm. It flattens out as it spreads, but instead of flattening into oblivion, it travels as a blob. That hill is betraying me. It won't vanish until it settles, and that's going to be—

"Against my house!"

I estimate I have about ten seconds before the House of Mediocrity meets the reaper. And it's almost night. I'll get caught with my pants at least halfway down.

I run past the tree farm and to the pond, equipping my pail, and fill it with water. It's not heavy at all and I can fully run now that the Fatigue is gone.

"Noooo!"

The lava's about to touch my farm, my beautiful barley plants. It edges my Compost Bin which catches fire. The smell of smoke fills the air and smoke blocks rise to the heavens. I up my pace, gasping for breath as I cross the grass and back into my yard. Somewhere a Dreadmoth screeches. Wait. It's straight ahead of me, fluttering over the glowing lava. They must be attracted to light.

Fantastic.

But apparently I'm more attractive than the lava because the fluttering wings and that green grimace dive right at me.

I backpedal as something hisses. My house. It's gone. Toast. I run back under a nearby tree, frustration quaking my chest. I'm going to lose my house and probably die. The Dreadmoth strikes the leaves of the tree with another screech and rustle. I fumble with my hotbar, forcing myself to focus. The Flint Hammer was a disaster. I'll try the Flint Hatchet. Something light. Something that won't have too much knockback.

I swing with the crappy weapon, damaging the Dreadmoth to the tune of more hissing sounds from the direction of my homestead. But it doesn't fly back super far, and I'm able to hack again and again. It must take me ten strikes, but at last the creature dies, dropping another Silk and two Dreadmoth Plates.

But I couldn't care less about that, because the rest of my progress is located in my house. I dart back to my dark yard and towards my fortress.

"What the heck?"

Only one flat polygon of lava remains, and as it touches my farm, it hisses and goes dark. The Compost Bin is gone, but the fire is out, and nothing is giving off light. No more Dreadmoths approach and I see nothing against the stars or the light of the pentagon moon that's rising over the trees.

Things are quiet.

My house...my house...is fine.

And amazingly, so is the garden that lava tried to destroy a few seconds ago. My barley still stands, ready for harvest.

I blink.

This doesn't make sense.

But since I still have no armor and am relishing not having Fatigue and low health, I run back, grab the Dreadmoth drops, and run back inside my mysteriously intact house to wait for morning. After stashing my Dried Clay Bricks and leftover Clay Globs into the Storage Crate, all that's left to do is wait. One of my windows looks out on my farm, and as the sun rises and damages a couple of nearby Ghouls, I can sort of see what happened.

The lava did reach my row of irrigated Fertile Soil farmland blocks.

And when it did, it turned into a row of flat, dark pentagons of what I'm guessing is basalt.

"Wow. That is some tough barley."

My crops acted as a wall against the lava, forcing it to cool and dry. My Compost Bin is gone, but that's no big deal. I'll make another.

Why the heck did my crops survive when my Compost Bin didn't?

After exiting the House of Mediocrity, I examine the farm and the dried lava. Maybe lava dries after flowing like that for a few seconds, but I find it odd it all dried when it touched the farm. The farmland almost acted like, well, water. The Fertile Farmland row has darkened even more since I placed it, indicating it's being fed by the single block of water I've put in the farm.

You're working on the farming, which should turn out to be a very good source of resources, and you're on your way to some mob traps.

Okay. Experimenting is in order.

* * * * *

After visiting my Swamp Ghoul farm and obtaining more Putrid Flesh, I make another couple of Compost Bins and place them between my house and the cliff. Once I've got more Fertile Soil, I place it not in the ground, but in the air, by sticking it to the edge of the cliff and creating a dumb-looking platform that stretches over my head. But hey, it's in the name of science.

Then I dig out the middle block, glad Fertile Soil drops as itself. I put a block of Common Dirt under the opening, create a dirt staircase up to the platform, and place my Wooden Pail of water into the middle hole. Then I hoe the Fertile Soil, turning it into farmland.

But this time, I plant nothing.

I just let the water permeate the soil. One by one, the farmland blocks darken a bit.

And then something new happens.

Running water.

I scramble down my dirt staircase to the sight of blue, pixelated water cascading down from each irrigated farmland block. The big, square waterfall remains as I wait and wait, and the water at the bottom spreads out several meters before stopping not far from the back of my house.

And I laugh.

Farmland acts like a water source block, a portable source of the stuff that never seems to run out so long as it's fed. That's why I didn't lose my farm and house last night.

"TheWattleman, you've done it again." This is a game changer.

CHAPTER NINETEEN

Over the next couple of days, I gladly play Salvosera from the moment I wake up to the time I get logged out automatically by the system (set to nine hours of gameplay, I find out on my own.) I'm kind of disappointed that Candi doesn't log me out herself and talk about grabbing dinner, but seeing as she seems to be the recruiter and also a tester, I understand.

Well, that's what I tell myself.

But I immerse myself in projects, knowing that I must be making Salvos happy.

On Friday I get out of bed after texting Natalie and telling her to have a good day at her job.

I hope so, she texts back.

I don't like that, but at least I can offer her real hope now. *I get paid today. And if I don't, I walk.*

I'm over the moon. Aside from the Lava Incident, I'm doing well. If I weren't, Candi would have showed up to let me know. Corporate shouldn't find any reason to kick me out.

I exit my apartment after nuking some breakfast, palms tingling as I contemplate my next mob trap. I walk downstairs and through the office area, passing the lounge.

The coffee machine isn't even bubbling yet. I'm up earlier than normal. When I reach the testing room, it's empty as usual. I've likely put in more hours than anyone this week.

Once in my suit, I get into the Salvos Simulator and log in.

And I spawn back in next to my improved Swamp Ghoul trap. Pushing myself off the ground, I first eye the flowing channel of water underneath the Glass Panes and the Common Leaves. A few Swamp Ghouls are already straying out of the dark room and dying, pushed by the new water currents I've placed inside the tower. Oh, and I've added two more levels to the trap, each with flowing water currents inside that both spawn and push Swamp Ghouls to their ultimate demise. I no longer have to deal with the Common Leaves since—tada—water doesn't flow down through vertical Glass Panes.

(Yes, it's an odd bug, but one I hope Salvos doesn't fix.)

"I never thought crap would get me this far," I mutter. "Mike, stop it with the bathroom humor. You're more sophisticated than that." But it's true. The worst blocks in the game always seem to be the most valuable.

And dozens of Putrid Flesh and Bones lie at the end of the water channel, washed into my reach from two more Fertile Farmland blocks. I seize the drops, glad I've discovered that spreading my fingers and making a huge grabbing motion picks up all of the same type of drop at once. Major time saver.

Then I run back to my house, watching the Scattered Woods for any stray Lavaworms or Dreadmoths. Nope. All clear. The sun climbs as my glorious new barley farm renders into view, nestled against the cliff and complete with its tiers and multiple waterfalls.

"And behold, the Mike Wattles Farm of Actual Productivity."

It wasn't a hard build. I just had to irrigate the top row of Fertile Farmland which unleashed a waterfall down each side of the tiered farm, which in turn irrigated the rest. It looks cool and since all the farmland I've got is the Fertile stuff, I've got food for life. Golden barley grows on row, which I harvest with my Flint Backhoe. It makes a satisfying crunching sound each time I swing it at the plants, which break and drop Barley Seeds and Bunches of Barley. Then I take my haul into my house, refine it into Barley Flour in my Crafting Tab, and run back outside to where my new Stone Brick Oven sits beside my second Clay Brick Oven.

"Okay," I say. "So it turns out that Stone Bricks are made by cooking stone in a Clay Oven. Peat Bricks are easy to make. Just stick Peat in a Brick Mold. Done." I circle my Ovens. "But as a fuel, they suck."

Yeah. Peat Bricks cook one item each. The only perk is that they light automatically when stuck into an Oven, and I can light my Peat Torches by touching them to the Oven, too. But at least they don't explode the Clay Oven or melt through it. And though the Stone Oven looks cooler than the Clay one, it's still one cook per Peat Brick.

Obviously better Ovens should be capable of using better fuels without blowing up in my face.

"What a long wait," I grumble, inserting my stack of Barley Flour. "I've got to find another fuel."

So far, none of the mobs have dropped any. I turn towards my second dirt skyscraper, the one on the other side of my house as the Ovens. It's identical to the Swamp Ghoul trap, but with a wooden tunnel housing the water stream that pushes mobs out. Well, that's *supposed* to push mobs out. Since I don't want to die, I've barricaded the end of the tunnel with Common Wood Slabs, which keeps the monsters in but allows me to hack at them.

And so far, that particular trap sucks, too.

"Yep." I peek inside to see the legs of one Common Ghoul. It jumps up and down against the slab barrier and makes its *sclorc* sound. What gives? It's the same setup as the other trap. Maybe the lower Hostility score here is playing a role, but during the day, more mobs should be spawning inside. I had a Lavaworm yesterday, which I killed for something called a Basaltic Rock, but nothing else dropped. And Dreadmoths? They fly, so water streams won't push them anywhere. And they probably need open sky to spawn since I've never heard them screeching underground. I've heard plenty of Ghouls under my feet, though.

Disappointing. I have a feeling their plates can be used for armor.

My crappy trap means that the game can find other, better spots for monsters to spawn in this area.

There just might be a massive dungeon or cave system under my feet that's taking all the mob spawns.

I don't waste my time on the Common Ghoul. I turn away, determined to do some exploration now that I've got forty Bread Loaves and sixty Lit Peat Torches in my inventory.

I've only begun to tap Salvosera.

And there's an opening to a cave not far from here. It's close to where I had my first encounter with a Lavaworm, somewhere to the left of my tree farm.

Gathering my stuff and leaving the Stone Brick Oven to take its sweet time cooking, I walk in that direction under the noon sun. The cave opening comes into view and my insides coil a bit looking at it. I can't see far inside. The cave itself slopes downward into oblivion, leaving Common Stone blocks to act as natural steps. At least I've brought plenty of Common Soil to make a staircase out if I need to.

"Here goes, Mike." I lower myself into a seated position and scramble downward.

CHAPTER TWENTY

Heart thumping, I double check to ensure I have my Lit Peat Torches as well as my Flint Hammer and Flint Hatchet in my hotbar. I keep my hotbar open in case I have to tap it in the hurry. I've tried to dual wield torches and a weapon, but so far that seems to be a feature Salvos hasn't added. So for now, I'm stuck wielding either a torch or a crap weapon. And if a Lavaworm jumps out at me I'll need to do the fastest switching I've ever done.

And I still have no armor.

"Awesome, Mike," I say as the light dims. The cave below spirals down, down, and out of view. "This is a great idea." How far down does it go? "This is why I like mob traps."

I scoot down one block, then another, then another. I look up to see that I've descended ten meters. The stone gets colder the farther I go down. A shiver runs through me. This is real. Creationist let you know you were in VR. Salvosera is a whole other ballgame.

And the first distant *sclorc* sounds from below. Then silence. Silence is bad. That means every other monster down there could be a Lavaworm.

The light dims. And that allows me to see farther into the cave since the sun isn't glaring into my face.

Well, I can see the floor, at least, flat and gray. There's a small drop before I get there and it's clear this entrance opens into some sort of catacomb or tunnel. Once I drop down there I ~~will probably get~~ could get mobbed from both directions. Once I reach the bottom of the cave entrance, I switch to the Common Dirt in my hotbar and place it, forming a staircase of four levels down to the floor.

It's dark down there.

Quiet.

I descend slowly, still seated like a coward, looking both ways into pure dark. I do not want to step onto the floor. Switching to my torches, I thrust my hand at the nearby stone on the floor, highlight it, and place one.

Peat Torches suck, too.

Peat just plain...sucks. Because the torch, which is just a stick, twine, and a glob of smoldering peat, barely gives off light and barely any flame. Well, the air smells a bit like smoke and I can see a few more blocks to my left.

Clearly there must be something better than Peat Torches, and it's down here. Coal, maybe. Peat Torches, like certain Internet browsers, are only useful for getting a better version.

Another *sclorc* sounds in the distance.

The longer I sit here, the more likely mobs will be to spawn and find me. I've figured out that they only spawn at least twenty blocks away. I've got to use that to my advantage.

So I take a breath. "Here goes." And I jump down from the staircase and run to the right, stepping over the low heat of the Peat Torch. I place another torch and then another, just five or so blocks apart, lighting the cave ahead just enough for me to progress. The walls are mostly gray, though I spot a few veins of a sparkling, orange and tan stone mixed with the Common Stone. I keep running, gasping for breath down the long, winding cave tunnel until I see the end and place a torch on the wall. It sticks to the wall without falling, just high enough to light the ceiling.

"No mobs," I mutter, relieved. I'd hate to think of what a cave in a high hostility area would look like. Then I turn my gaze upward at the ceiling of the cave. Three polygons of Common Stone catch my eye. Yellow-orange splotches on them tell me I've found some sort of ore, like the green one I haven't been able to mine back at the cliff.

Palms tingling, I take my Flint Hammer and hack, praying this ore's Resistance isn't higher than two. Cracks form across the ore as I hack, and it breaks and drops to the floor as a sparkling yellow-orange sprite, shaped like a shard. I tap it to pick it up, and since this part of the cave is now safe, I check my inventory.

Spark Cluster
Resistance: 2

Fall Damage: +2

Gravity: 0

Speed: 0

Refinable: 1

"So this is how you start making better torches." I think of my Flint Chisel back home, the one tool I haven't used yet, and I know how to get something useful out of this stuff.

Sclorc.

I jump.

So much for safety first.

A squishing sound rings out right next to me, and I whirl, raising my Flint Hammer. A Common Ghoul has appeared right in front of me, and then a second drops out of a hole in the ceiling that I missed.

"Really?" I let out a curse and jump back, swinging, and pressure runs up my arms as I hit both Ghouls at once. The brown creatures fall back, stunned, and I swing again and again until they fall over, dead, and vanish into those puffs of dust. Then I scramble, equipping my Common Soil which I use to plug the hole in the ceiling, a hole that could lead to a vast cavern for all I know. "Just what I needed was a jumpscare." But I'm secretly glad for it. I was beginning to think that caving would be too easy.

I quickly dig out the rest of the Spark Ore, which turns out to be a vein of eight (yes!) and I progress to the orange, sparkling rock I saw earlier in the cave. That turns out to be Granite, and it's also refinable but deals increased fall damage (+ 4.) I mine that, too. That might be good for some falling traps and possibly even for tool making. I haven't gotten Common Stone to work as an ingredient in any tools and I'm willing to try anything to reach the higher tiers.

After mining another vein of Spark Ore, I eye my Common Soil staircase. I'm back to where I started. Gross footsteps sound somewhere in the darkness, but they're distant, and a brief crackling noise tells me a Lavaworm has fallen and taken damage about an equal distance away. I progress past my staircase, tiptoeing and placing Crap Torches along the wall until my heart leaps into my throat and I stop.

Sheer terror grips me. What the heck? I wobble in place, waving my arms, trying to stop myself from falling forward. Once still, I blink and realize that I'm standing on the edge of a massive drop-off.

I back off. "Well, that explains it."

An expanse of darkness stretches out in front of me, and the breeze hitting my face from all directions tells me I've stumbled on a *huge* cavern. My eyes adjust and I spot a faint light far below, maybe from a pool of lava, and the shape of a Lavaworm jumping in front of it. Wet footsteps sound down below as the *sclorcs* of excited, hungry Ghouls ring out below me. Tapping footsteps, a sound I've never heard, ring out from everywhere, turning to a skittering as what sounds like a million insects rush for my location.

I backpedal as my heart leaps into my throat.

A new mob.

Great.

Can they climb walls?

I turn around and I run, knowing why my second mob trap isn't getting many spawns. All the monsters are down here.

And I scramble up the dirt staircase as the skittering gets closer. Whatever's chasing me is able to climb walls. Awesome.

"Go, Mike. Go!"

But I already know that I won't make it out of the cave in time to avoid it. Climbing out of the cave will take too long. I turn once in the entrance tunnel, bathed in the pale light from the sky, and I wait for the new monster to scale the dirt steps.

And it does. A segmented, brown centipede with nasty pinchers leaps at me before I have time to swear. My view flashes red as my health bar shrinks to almost half. I swing my hammer again, hitting the mastiff-sized monster as it lands at my feet. Pressure spreads across my chest as the "pain" registers. I back up and swing again, catching the jumping centipede midair, and the creature makes a faint gasping noise and another series of clicking sounds as it falls over and dies. It drops some Silk and a brown plate, which I seize.

And then the pressure on my chest, where it bit me, starts to burn as I climb back towards the sunlight, taking one level at a time. Another status effect appears in the top right of my vision, and this one's a green droplet.

Poison.

"Get out of here," I tell myself as the feeling intensifies.

My Calories bar drops, but at least I have plenty of Bread Loaves in my hotbar. I sit down on an outcrop halfway up the entrance since nothing else is coming after me and I eat quickly, almost choking on the chewy dough. I've got to regenerate my health. If I don't, I'm going to die.

But my health refuses to rise. Instead, it drops a little more.

"So that's what Poison does," I grumble, climbing out of the cave and straightening to find the sun sinking, already close to the horizon. "I can't heal."

But before I can rush back to my house so I don't get murdered, everything goes black. At first I think it's the Poison effect, but then I'm falling backwards through a void. The burning feeling disappears.

Someone's logging me out. And I've only been in the game for a couple of real life hours. That doesn't make sense.

When I find myself in the Salvos Simulator, I pull off my helmet, get my bearings, and turn towards the door.

But no one is there. My door's open a bit, though.

"What the heck?" I'm still reeling from my experience in the cave. Did I screw up? Now a new terror fills my chest. Someone must have logged me out. That's clear.

I take a breath, determined to figure out why.

I don't even bother to get changed. Leaving the helmet on the floor beside the Simulator, I leave the blue lights behind and walk towards the lounge, where I expect to find someone. But as soon as I turn the corner to the office area, I spot two people walking into the fancy meeting room: Candi, dressed in a black suit, and someone I've only seen in online footage of gaming conventions.

Anthony Anton.

The CEO of Salvos. The piebald head and the bushy eyebrows betray the fact that it's him.

He enters the meeting room as Candi holds open the door for him like a dutiful servant. And though she should clearly be able to see me standing here at the corner, she pays me no attention as she closes the door behind her, leaving me a clear invitation to eavesdrop.

CHAPTER TWENTY-ONE

Resisting is futile. It's clear Candi logged me out and ran, hoping I'd figure out the cue. My heart pounds. Why would she do this? It's clear that whatever is going to take place in that meeting room is important and she wants me to know about it.

My heart pounds in my ears. Anthony Anton is a founding member and the CEO of Salvos Corporation. The big cheese. The guy who imagined Creationist and blew up the whole sandbox genre of gaming. I can't just go over there and press my ear to the door.

The door stays shut. Chairs squeak inside.

If I'm caught—

This hallway has none of those black spheres on the ceiling. I see no evidence of security cameras. I eye the hallway for any other signs of them.

I'm not seriously going to do it.

Yes, I am.

I nudge shut the door to the lounge most of the way, careful not to make any noise, just in case there are cameras in there. It's right across from the meeting room.

Okay. I'm doing this. Feeling like scum, I press my ear to the door. At least they're seated and those chairs make noise. Once someone gets up, I can easily get back to the testing room before I'm noticed.

"Candace," Anthony starts in a neutral tone, letting silence drag out. It's clear he wants her to speak first, and he's making it sound like she has to answer for something.

I tense. That's not like him. At gaming conventions, he's always smiling, though distant, and waving to Creationist fans. One time he posed with a life-size statue of a Phantom and circulated the picture on social media. The man in the meeting room is all business.

"We now have seven testers in total," Candi says a moment later. "Matt is a great builder and I've sent you the streams of the city he's creating. Don's found almost all of the biomes except for the Glimmer. And Liz is almost done exploring that vast cavern she found. Oh, and my projects should be ready for when the next phase begins."

My palms tingle. So far, it seems that Candi and Anthony are alone. None of the other founders have come to this meeting.

"Yes. They are all very impressive and I would expect no less out of them, and especially you," Anthony says. "However, we do have seven testers, and we at corporate have determined that we would like to have five on staff when Salvosera comes out of closed beta."

I cup my ear. *We have seven.* They want to go down to five soon?

Is this what Candi wants me to hear?

Is Anton deciding our futures today?

Miriam, the assistant, did handle my contract, not Anton. Anton never agreed to pay me and now he's bound by law. And probably not happy that someone went over his head.

"We have Kevin and Val, who haven't had much of a chance to show their skill sets yet," Candi says. "Kevin is about to stumble upon the Elixir system, I believe. And Val has begun exploring the mechanics of Magical Wares."

I let out a very slow breath. Salvosera has a magical system and an elixir system? I've barely tapped this game.

"That is true. I have seen the streams," Anthony says. He's getting impatient. "At least our newest closed beta tester is finally showing some promise. He's only died once, but I have to admit he's made some clumsy mistakes."

I gulp, knowing exactly what he means. He saw the Lava Incident and probably didn't like the House of Mediocrity, or my brush with the centipede monster, or my ugly Common Soil structures. He probably watched as I lugged that heavy lava Pail all the way back to my base, cursing his name. I didn't wish death on him out loud, did I?

Anyway, I've just gotten confirmation that I am not the favorite around here.

"All of the players have made mistakes," Candi says. I hear the tension in her voice. She's not used to standing up to Anthony, then, and I wish I could help her with her position. "That's part of learning the game mechanics and part of closed beta testing. Say, do you have an ETA for the next beta version? We still have a bit of feedback to gather from the testers tonight which I'll send over right away."

Thank you for changing the subject, I think.

"The developers are not entirely sure when that date will be, but the release will happen some time before the end of the month. It will depend on how much feedback we receive," Anthony says. "But the general plan is still the same. Beta 1.1 will hopefully fix some bugs and balance issues, and Beta 1.2 will mark the start of Salvosera's GameTube presence. Our marketing department has requested that five of our beta testers stay on as paid streamers, under our account, and that is a number that I agree with."

"Five streamers?" Candi asks. "We have seven testers, including myself, and all of them have something to contribute." She leaves the meaning hanging.

My heart leaps into my throat. Five streamers. They're going to let two of us go soon. And I know my head is on the chopping block, as Landon used to warn his employees back at the call center.

How much longer do I have here? I know the testing period is temporary, of course, but once Beta 1.1 comes out, Beta 1.2—the version we won't all stay here to see— will follow soon after.

And that'll probably be right when Natalie's problems level up to 50.

"Yes. I am aware," Anthony says. "We will be using Beta 1.1 to determine which of our testers will continue to 1.2. The first two to die during the Beta 1.1 period will be excluded from continuing to the paid status. They will be moved out of the headquarters immediately to avoid alerting the other testers of the new conditions."

"Do the contracts allow for this?" Candi asks.

"Yes, of course. There is the special obligations clause which states that players who fail to meet their special obligations can be removed from the program at any time."

Anton sounds happy. Confident.

And I'm starting to shake as a hollow feeling fills my chest. Yes. There *is* a special obligations clause in the contract. I dimly remember it.

"But all players have died," Candi says, not daring to let another uncomfortable pause drag out. She forces a laugh. "Some of our testers are reliant on the money and shelter we provide them."

"Candace, it is not Salvos Corporation's fault that some people have failed to save and invest and can't help their families with expenses. I know there are plenty of charitable organizations out there who will help these people."

I almost rip myself from the door.

This is *not* Anton, the smiling man with the Phantom statue. The man who brought Creationist to the world. The man who organized CreationCon every single year for the past decade.

Only it is.

"Our testers are a team," Candi says, voice rising. "Losing even one member may lower morale."

"That will not happen," Anton says. "It's necessary to cull the herd. If we have too many testers streaming Salvosera to the public, demand for these streams will drop, and so will revenue. We can't give away too many details about the game. Our marketing department has advised us that we should only keep the best revenue generators. Keep the supply low, and demand will rise."

Pain in my palms steals my attention to the fact that I'm digging my fingernails into them. Pure rage seizes every muscle in my body and makes my teeth hurt. Does he know about my sister? Miriam might have mentioned it when Anton grilled her for agreeing to pay me. He just might know...he just might know...

"So, when will Salvosera go live to the public?" Candi asks as if she can sense that I'm about to go Mr. Hyde and bust down the door.

"We are aiming for six months. That will give us plenty of time to build buzz in the public," Anthony continues, his tone going from confident to chipper. "Everyone will be dying to visit our Salvos Centers to play Salvosera. To buy a subscription. To get their hands on a Salvos suit. People will travel to have this experience. And once revenue jumps, we will be expanding out to smaller communities and rural areas."

My pulse roars in my ears. I can see Anton salivating all over the table.

The Creationist icon that I once admired is just another Landon, only worse, because he's a millionaire with real power.

I barely realize when the conversation shifts to Candi's method of gathering feedback and her use of the company credit card. From there, it shifts to petty stuff like the weather. I tear myself from the door, go get changed, and then walk back through the hallway to the apartment elevator. Once upstairs in the apartment lobby, I find Don and a young woman—probably Liz or Val—chatting by the elevator. The young woman has hair made of winding, copper, blond, and black braids and she's one of the shortest women I've ever seen.

"Hey," Don says "Did you hear? Feedback meeting tonight."

"Feedback meeting," I say. Salvos has to figure out how to kill the less desirable of us off.

And I can't say anything.

"Yeah. Every Friday," Don says. "They cater so it's not bad." He gives me an oblivious thumbs-up.

The last thing I want is food after listening to Anthony talk. I open my mouth, but the woman eyes the ceiling. Yeah. Another black orb is up there. So I plaster a stupid smile on my face.

"I'll be there." I nod. "Pizza sounds great. I'll write down some notes on things I think can be improved." At least I have a slight advantage there.

"Just be careful," the woman says. "We're not supposed to share anything with each other and well, you'll see. I'm Val, by the way."

"Good to meet you, Val," I say. I can tell she's a firecracker and she's barely opened her mouth.

I head to my apartment, in no mood to go back into the game yet or to chat with my fellow testers. Rude, yeah, but my gut is giving me tons of warning signals. I storm back into my room, tearing off the memo on my door that gives me the time and place for the feedback meeting tonight, and I toss it down next to my contract.

What if I die during Beta 1.1?

Absently, I stand at the kitchen counter and thumb through the contract, folding the corners and straightening them out again. Why did I trust that this would work out, that this was the opportunity Dad said would come to me?

Page one. Page two. Page three. Then page six.

Huh?

I jolt as I go through the pages again, eyeing the gray numbers that are barely legible thanks to the printer being low on ink. Yeah. There's no page four or five in this contract. They screwed up.

My gut clenches tighter. *Or did they?*

"Really?" I thumb through the contract again, reading it to see if something sounds cut off and omitted between page three and six, but it all looks okay. My gut screams again, turning over, as I think of a horrifying possibility.

What if there is a page four and five, and Salvos just didn't show them to me? What if Salvos has a contract on file that has my signature, along with those pages that I've never seen?

And how would I prove it?

I swear and slap the contract back down on the counter. What did I sign, exactly, and what did I get myself into?

CHAPTER TWENTY-TWO

For the first time since arriving at Salvos's apartment complex, I take a walk around downtown Charlotte. I've already met my 20-hour quota for the week, but my head is spinning so much that I know if I try to play my world right now, I'll mess something up royally.

Man, I'm an idiot.

I pull my old hoodie over my head even though it's hot, drawing suspicious stares from people on the street. It's just after lunch from what I can tell. People in business suits and blouses exit restaurants and fast food places, busy with their own worries. I do not blend in. I can smile at someone and send them running.

Not that I've ever been super social, anyway.

And not that I care. I've got a target on my back.

I think about calling Natalie but she's got to be at work and off her lunch break. So instead I walk into a random fast food place I've never visited and order a drink with my pocket change. I should get paid today. The thought sends a wave of nausea through me as I exit the fast food place, ditching my half-finished drink in a trash can. Leaning against a building, I check my bank account through my phone's app. For all I know there's a clause in the completed contract about not paying me if I so much as fart in the apartment.

Your Balance: $3,212.

My jaw drops.

I've been paid.

Salvos actually kept their end of the deal.

I sag with relief against the building. Maybe I'm overreacting and the missed numbers on the contract were just a typo.

"Wait, Mike," I say. "Don't trust them." I still have the update to worry about and my best shot at surviving that is to see if I can squeeze some info about it out at the group dinner. It's at five—four hours from now—so I have time to think about how to approach it. And with my mind still working, I continue my long walk around downtown.

* * * * *

We all actually meet in the same big meeting room I put my ear up to earlier. As I enter five to five, it smells of heavenly food. A worker wearing a green apron for a fancy Italian place lines up aluminum trays of awesomeness on the counter. I spot Don already loading up on salad and breadsticks while Matt's seated, a heaping plate in front of him. Val and the other woman, Liz, sit together and a guy I haven't seen before, a real hardcore geek complete with thick glasses, waves. Everyone seems friendly enough.

"This is Kevin," Don says, slugging the new guy on the shoulder. "Oh. And this is Liz." Liz too is a fellow geek, with a plaid shirt with a Vox tee underneath.

We all shake hands and settle down to dinner. We all eat in silence and I sense that like the rest of the facility, the meeting room is bugged. Dystopia, here we come. Anthony Anton has probably already left in his private jet. After all, it's Candi's job to collect feedback. And why should Anton talk to us revenue generators?

At last, as dinner's drawing to a close, our final beta tester enters the room. Candi offers a small wave as she struts over to the food and loads up, along with two new suited people who have come in with her. Neither is Anton.

"Everyone," she says. "Thank you for your feedback so far on Salvosera. Mike, I know you haven't had a chance to do this yet, but this is how it works. Everyone will write their feedback on a card, separately, and turn it in. It's kind of an essay." She frowns at me and I read meaning in that stare. Yes. She was trying to warn me about what's coming.

"Got it," I say. I'm mentioning the issue with the lava pail for sure. No player will like that feature. And how some crafting recipes are almost too easy, which goes against the theme of Salvosera so far. But should I do that with Anton out to kill me?

He *has* to be out to kill me. I'm the troublemaker.

She doesn't miss a beat even though she's got bags under her eyes. Candi turns to the two suits who came in with her. "Please welcome Robbie Cratt, marketing genius for Salvos, and his wife Lisa, who is leading the development team."

A bit of applause rises from the table. I have to force myself to clap. They're another pair of big names from Salvos, and I don't know how they feel about us. The couple is young, maybe in their upper thirties, and the guy is well-built. And isn't Lisa Anton's daughter? She has his thick eyebrows, that's for sure.

Lisa steps forward, almost nudging Candi aside. "We are pleased to announce that Beta 1.1 will roll out to you to Monday. Our dev team is working tirelessly to bring it to you over the weekend."

Now cheers rise. Kevin claps over his head and Val slaps her hand to her mouth. I sense my back prickling. Do they know I suspect something fishy is going on?

"That's awesome. What's in this patch?" I blurt.

Lisa laughs, a high-pitched, annoying sound. "We are not at liberty to say. It will be your job, as beta testers, to test the waters."

I'm afraid of that. I swallow but force myself to keep on that stupid smile. This is the version meant to kill those of us Anton doesn't like.

No one else asks questions. I'm the new guy and it's showing. At least that's expected of me. Robbie steps forward next.

"Beta 1.1 will be the unofficial end to the rough side of the closed beta," he says. "This is the time for us to work out the last major bugs and balance issues. It is true that Beta 1.1 has a few new features, but they shouldn't have too much impact on gameplay. After Beta 1.1 comes to an end, we will be hiring on paid streamers to bring Salvosera to the public for the first time."

Gasps sound around the table as Liz once again slaps her hand to her mouth. Don grabs the table and Matt leans forward.

But still, no one asks any questions, least of all how much they'd make.

"We want several streamers to be willing to stream live on GameTube for several hours per day. Get the public excited. Bring your shining personalities to the world," Robbie continues. "That's how Creationist exploded in popularity. This, combined with us rolling back support for Creationist over the next several months, will drive gamers towards Salvosera."

"You're going to stop supporting Creationist altogether?" I blurt. The most popular game in the world? I remember Candi saying something about me being lucky I didn't go in that direction.

"Yes," Robbie says with an award-winning smile. "We are confident that this move will help drive subscriptions for Salvosera. You have to understand that Creationist is going on its eleventh year. The player base is ready for a new, next-generation experience."

I swallow. I know full well Salvosera will be pricey and while Creationist will still exist for a long time, players will get bored without any new patches or new features to look forward to. And some of them won't be able to afford the jump to Salvosera right away. But I don't think this is the time to argue my case.

"This is awesome," Val says. She looks to Liz who's also grinning. I can't even tell them that not all of us will make the cut.

And if I do, will they believe me? I'm the only skeptic here.

"So be sure to fill in your cards after dinner," Lisa says, once again taking the stage. "Your feedback is valuable and will shape Salvosera for years to come."

The two leave and I expect Candi to sit down with us and speak to us alone. But instead, she takes two bites with her plastic fork, turns, and exits the room, almost as if she's following Lisa and Robbie.

"Wow. This is our lucky break," Don tells me.

"Yeah. Maybe they'll finally add a multiplayer server where we can actually do some PVP and challenge each other to arena combat," Kevin adds. He and Val look at each other, grinning.

I look at my nearly-empty plate of food, shocked I managed to eat with the news I got today.

"I've got to go use the bathroom," I say, rising.

No one questions why I leave. I throw out my dinner roll and hope they blame a gluten allergy. Robbie and Lisa have vanished, probably to go talk over in the testing room, but Candi's in the lounge, reaching into the minibar.

I walk in. "Hey."

Candi whirls. She's got a small shot glass in her hand and her food in the other. The bags under her eyes have darkened.

"Look," she says, then lets silence drag out.

I don't know what to say. If she's not sending out distress signals, I don't know what she's doing. "Everyone's excited." I force a smile, knowing full well there must be cameras on us.

"So am I," she says, letting a hint of sarcasm slip between her words. "Oh. Everyone goes into the little office to fill out their cards. By the way, it's one at a time in there. And I agree that the lava pail thing needs to be fixed. It's part of the Fatigue debuff, but still very annoying as people will need to cook to replenish their Calories bar."

"Uh..." I start, but Candi walks past me, leaving her glass on the counter.

I stand there, stung, as she stalks back into the meeting room across the hall.

"What the heck?" I whisper to myself.

There's something going on under the surface, a surface that I can barely scratch.

CHAPTER TWENTY-THREE

My dinner churns in my stomach once I get up to my new apartment. As soon as I cross the threshold, lost in thoughts about why Candi is sending me such mixed signals, my phone buzzes.

Probably Natalie. I stop and let out a breath. Of course Candi is sending me mixed signals. Salvos is watching her every move. She has no choice but to pretend to blow me off, right?

I pull out my phone. Yeah. It's Natalie. Mom and Dad don't check on me that often which I understand because Natalie's the one who's sick.

Hey Mike.

Boss wants a meeting one on one Monday. Just thought you should know.

I curse and sit down on my bed. Monday? Seriously? The jerk is going to let Natalie worry about this all weekend? Talk about a power move. I think of her sitting home, scared to go out and spend any money and scared about the future. The more I think about it, the less I'm sure who I hate more: Anthony Anton or her boss. But I text her back before thinking.

What's your boss's address?

She responds. *LOL.*

Then I get an idea. There's nothing in my contract about not having people over, is there? Of course, I can't be sure, but Natalie should not spend the weekend alone.

I turn and leave my apartment. My time here might be very limited, so if there's any time to try my idea, it's now.

* * * * *

"Are you kidding?" Natalie walks into my apartment the next morning. "This is awesome, Mike. You did well!" My sister opens the white curtains and looks out on the skyline. "The view. This place must be worth at least two grand a month."

"And it's free," I tell her. "You, by the way, are free to crash here whenever you want."

Natalie turns and wraps her thin arms around me. Like me, she's tall, almost lanky, and has a curtain of dark hair. Natalie's got bags under her eyes now. She's a bit pale and I can tell she's not feeling the best, but she's holding up against her first treatment well. My sister is strong and I know she'll make it.

But if she can't pay—

I have to hold on. I have to make it to streamer status in Beta 1.2.

"I might have to take you up on it," Natalie says, closing the curtains. She eyes my old Virtual World platform and headset which I've got sitting on the floor next to the TV and laptop. I haven't used it since getting here. "You're not getting rusty in Creationist, are you?"

"I hope not." I eye the front door, waiting. I've got a surprise for her, a surprise I worked on all last night.

Natalie puts her own Virtual World platform down next to mine. "So, you set up a multiplayer server? Anything special?"

"Nope. Just a regular old multiplayer server. Fresh world. Open experience." I let an evil grin spread across my face. "We're not going to log in and play quite yet. Oh, and I ordered six pizzas. They'll be here in an hour."

"Six pizzas?" Her eyes widen. "But we can't eat that all. Mike, what are you up to?" Now she narrows her eyes at me.

"You'll see."

A knock on the door follows, and I maintain my grin as I answer it.

And on the other side stands Matt, Don, Val, Liz, and Kevin. Don waves and offers a sheepish smile. So other than tackling people and kidnapping them, he's shy in real life.

"Oh, cool. Are these your new friends?" Natalie asks.

She's oblivious. I haven't dared tell her who, exactly, my fellow testers are. But once we log in, she's in for a treat.

"They sure are," I said, letting in the small parade of people. Everyone's brought their own Virtual World platform and gear, and in typical geek fashion, we've got our names on our stuff via pieces of masking tape (me), name tag stickers (Hi! My name is Don), and even glittery cat stickers (Val.) A series of handshakes and first-name intros follow, though Matt offers a fist bump instead. Liz gives Natalie a hug.

I check the hallway outside, but one tester hasn't shown up.

I sigh. Of course. It's my hope that Candi is just busy working on those projects she said she'd have done before Monday. I feel like I'll never unravel the mystery of her. I'd been hoping she'd show up. I left a note on her apartment door last night with Liz's help. She and Natalie would get along.

The pizzas arrive a bit later and we all make small talk while we eat, seated in a circle on the floor. No one talks about Salvosera. Everyone's obeying the non-disclosure agreement and Natalie's eyes burn with curiosity, but she doesn't ask. That's fine.

We're about to log into my new server.

Once we're done eating and fighting food comas, the seven of us gear up. I step onto my platform, palms tingling with excitement.

Once Creationist's screen comes up, I choose my new world and activate voice chat. The voices of my fellow gamers fill my ears. My screen goes dark, and I half-expect to fall through a void, but Creationist isn't as immersive as Salvosera. I appear in a Wooded Wastelands biome, an area with a gray sky, yellow grass, and scattered graves, and Natalie appears beside me in her blocky elf warrior skin. She waves. "Hey, Mike." Her playername displays over her head: *ElfQueen546.*

The next person appears beside us. *Comma_Volt.* He's complete with his futuristic suit and goggles that he uses during his GameTube episodes. He hasn't changed it since starting his long journey to the Glitch Lands.

Natalie turns to him. "What?" she asks, confused.

"It's Don," he says, all humble.

"Are you the guy walking to the Glitch lands?" Natalie's voice rises.

Then Val logs in as *PrincessKitty21.* "Hey," she says with a blocky wave. Her cat skin smiles at Natalie.

"You're the PVP cat," Natalie says. "I've seen you play!"

Then Matt logs in as *NotBobTheBuilder* and gets another shocked reaction from Natalie, who turns in a circle and says something about his Mayan city. Kevin follows, logging in as *Meatboy529*, and finally Liz joins as *Flora_Explora.*

My sister lets out a squeal of disbelief as she finds herself surrounded by five famous Game Tubers.

And me.

"Are you kidding?" Natalie asks. "Don't tell me I'm expected to kill all of you. Or that we're being recorded. Mike, you hit the jackpot of a lifetime. I'm so jealous."

"Hey," Liz says. "We just want to have fun today and play a normal game. As friends. With no one watching us."

"What do you want to do first?" Matt asks as his hard-hat guy avatar looks around. "I don't like this spot for building, so I think we should find another. There's not much inspiration here."

"And nothing to explore," Liz adds.

"Yeah. It's kind of blah. The Wasteland Woods biome is always so flat," Natalie agrees. "Mike. You have got to get me into this. Tell them to take a look at my GameTube channel." Despite her treatment, she sounds more alive than I've ever heard her.

I gulp because Salvos already has two PVP players and there's only one way Natalie will ever have a ghost of a chance. But I have to try for her. "I will," I promise. "Now, let's figure out where to build our awesome base and have fun this weekend."

CHAPTER TWENTY-FOUR

The weekend with Natalie is awesome. We can almost forget that her boss has called her in for a one on one Monday. But when Sunday afternoon rolls around, I can tell she's getting nervous, and she talks a lot less with us over video chat. Instead, she focuses on exploring an abandoned castle in Creationist by herself, which worries me.

But I don't offer her any false hope. I know better. Kevin tells her to apply for short term disability, just as I've done, but he doesn't understand the setup going on at her office. I don't dare talk about my money on the server and I feel slimy about it. It's not as if I can. Candi's the only one who knows, and possibly Don.

When Natalie's ready to leave Sunday night to go back home, she hugs everyone.

"It was awesome," she says.

"We should get together again next weekend," Val says, stickered helmet under her arm. "You're a good player."

Natalie blushes. I give her a hug, too, and a pat on the back to remind her that I've got money I can send her.

But for how long?

I haven't told her about the possibility I won't be here much longer, and that Salvos has put a target on my back.

Once left alone, my apartment feels very, very quiet, and I'm exhausted from being on the Virtual World platform for almost two days straight. I drift off and wake the next morning. It's raining. Of course. Fat drops beat against the window and my whole apartment is bathed in gray. I want to roll over and fall back asleep but my bedside clock says that it's nine-thirty.

Natalie just might be in her meeting by now.

And I wait, because there's no way I'm going to be logged into Salvosera while she's in distress.

I walk to the kitchen and choke down some leftover pizza that tastes like cardboard. Natalie still doesn't get back to me. A meeting shouldn't take too long if her boss just wanted rid of her, right?

At last, she texts me.

Can't talk much. I can't take another day off or I'm gone. Not feeling good.

Hang in there. I've got your back if it goes south.

Already told Mom and Dad. Thanks because they don't have room.

True. Mom and Dad moved into a small, cozy cottage once Natalie and I got out. Being retired, they just can't help anymore. Besides, they're comfortable now. They served their time. Natalie and I are just getting started.

I swallow, debating on what to tell her. *I'm not sure how long I'll make money here.*

Oh, totally understand.

A weight comes off my chest and allows me to take a breath. But we both know what'll happen if I don't stay here. Natalie's life will be ruined because she won't have a choice but to rack up medical debt. And then what for? She could lose her home. Or she'd put off getting treatment.

I toss my half-eaten cold pizza and go downstairs, taking the elevator to the basement level. I slide my keycard, issued the night I got moved in, and unlock the steel door. Already, someone—probably Val judging from the tiny frame—is in a Salvos Simulator, embroiled in a fight. I tense, watching her, waiting for her to fall back and die, not knowing it would end her budding career. Then I remember and let out a breath. Val's Princess Kitty. She has a following from playing all those PVP arenas. She won't have a problem taking her following with her when Salvosera blows up and Creationist is left to die, even if Salvos stops supporting her.

But me, on the other hand—

I have to log in and make sure I'm not completely screwed. I left off at the mouth of that doom cave. Breaking a sweat, I watch as Val triumphs over whatever she's fighting and bends over, catching her breath. I get changed into my Salvos Suit, shocked no one else is down here yet to check out 1.1, and get into the box. Once I close the door behind me, the login process begins, and everything turns black as a tingle washes over my body.

No screen appears to tell me that I'm now in Beta 1.1. I find myself seated at the mouth of Death Cave. The sun is just rising, and I jump up when I see a Common Ghoul taking damage from the light and turning to attack me. I backpedal, making sure no Lavaworms are sneaking up behind me. So mobs have spawned here while I was logged out. Great. The world keeps going even when I'm not in it.

The Common Ghoul dies.

But that might be a good thing.

I bolt through the Scattered Woods which appear to be the same until I reach my house. The beautiful tower of dirt rises on the other side of it while my waterfall farm bursts with matured Barley crop. Good. My Calories bar is depleted and I once again have the Fatigue debuff. I need to eat. But at least the Poison is gone.

I've got twenty percent of my health left, give or take a few measly percentage points. My status bars won't drop from my view, urging me to pay attention. I bolt into the house, unwilling to take any chances. The Loaves are still in my hotbar from my mostly-failed cave run, so I eat two, savoring the flakiness. My health recovers and fills and the annoying tremble leaves my knees. Whew. That encounter with the toxic centipede thing cut my life way too close.

I can't die again.

But I also can't make zero progress.

Right now, they could be watching me.

Without asking I know I'm expected to figure out some awesome way to conquer that cave and turn it into a super successful mob farm, and I can see no way into it without, well, dying. I eye my crappy trap near the house and to my shock, the legs of two Common Ghouls and the coil of a Lavaworm jump up and down against the end slabs. Maybe 1.1 tweaked the spawning a bit and that could work in my favor. Or these mobs spawned while I was logged out. Of course Salvos's *only* goal won't be to destroy the troublemaker. They've got to balance the game.

"Finally." I go outside, head over, and kill the three mobs, who are all dumb and don't see me through the slabs.

The Lavaworm is tough and takes me five hits with my Flint Hatchet to kill. It's my first time killing one by hand. It dies with a crackle and drops two dark gray blocks and two Spark Clusters.

"Awesome. Spark Clusters are renewable energy."

Lavaworms drop Basaltic Rock, it turns out, and two Spark Clusters. Useful. So this Spark stuff is renewable and if it comes out of Lavaworms, flammable.

"I'll need some sort of auto killer on this trap. Then at least it will be cool." I can drown them by placing one of those irrigated Fertile Farm blocks in the right place, maybe.

That reminds me. I run back inside with my new prizes. My Flint Chisel combined with Spark Clusters in my Crafting Tab turns each Cluster into a Spark Brick. I end up with twenty in total. The Granite is also refinable.

Great. I can experiment and look productive while I think about how to *really* progress.

I eye my new Clay Oven and Stone Brick Oven, both of which still sit outside for safety reasons. After some experimenting with fuel bricks, I learn a few new things:

1.) Clay Ovens can handle Peat Bricks. That's it. They cook one item per brick. Spark Clusters make Clay Ovens explode, though you get about three seconds of ominous rumbling before that happens.

2.) Turns out Stone Brick Ovens handle Spark Clusters just fine, and each Cluster cooks or smelts two items.

3.) Granite Chunks can be smelted into Granite Bricks, and each piece of Granite yields two Granite Chunks. Honestly, I can't grasp the reasoning behind that, but Creationist lets you make tools out of Monster Eyes and even weirder things, so it's an improvement in the logic department.

4.) Basaltic Rock can be smelted into Basaltic Bricks. I just have two of those now, but I have the feeling I've figured out which type of oven can handle lava.

I'm not going to check to see if the lava bucket issue has been fixed yet, because that's a long walk and for all I know, Salvos has made lava capable of burning through Clay Pails. It would match the oven, at least. Check that. They probably *have* made that change after watching my embarrassing trek home. So lava will wait.

Since I'm down to two Spark Clusters, I'll have to wait for more Lavaworms in my trap. So far, there are none. The spawning hasn't been increased that much. That means the Death Cave.

"I need armor," I say. "That's the only way forward."

I've got three Dreadmoth Plates and four Silk. I arrange them in different formations in my Crafting Tab, but nothing happens no matter what I try. This stuff has to have a use. Then, at last, I check and find that the Dreadmoth Plate is refinable. But how?

Turns out I can cook Dreadmoth Plates. I use my last two pieces of Spark Ore to cook them into Hardened Dreadmoth Plates which are darker green, shiny versions of the original. I pull them out of the Stone Brick Oven's GUI and open my inventory and Crafting Tab again.

And I arrange an upside-down triangle of Hardened Dreadmoth Plates. Nothing happens, so I add two Silk above the bottom two Plates.

And lo and behold, a dark green, pixelated helmet appears in the output. It's even got a dark grimace across the front that looks awesome.

My jaw drops.

I have my first piece of armor.

I just might survive Beta 1.1.

The problem is, I've got a lot of Dreadmoths to kill before I get an entire set of armor.

CHAPTER TWENTY-FIVE

And what's even more awesome?

Dreadmoth spawns have been nerfed. That in-game night, I only see one distant Dreadmoth against the fading light of the setting sun. The rest of the night is filled with Lavaworms and Common Ghouls, and one Swamp Ghoul that wanders all the way up from the Northern Swamp. I stay in my house even though I'm wearing my new Plate Helmet. A single helmet isn't going to protect me much; I know that. In fact, wearing it has only filled about five percent of my silver Armor bar.

The sun rises, and the one distant Dreadmoth despawns.

I gulp. If Dreadmoths are less common, Salvos probably decided to balance that by making them tougher. And there's only one way to get an answer for that theory.

"That's going to suck," I say, letting my head thump to my window.

I guess I shouldn't complain after my last two encounters with those green, grimacing monsters that spit acid. But now I need some freaking armor before I face certain death.

I also need to stay long enough to convince Candi that Salvos should give Natalie a shot. I haven't seen her all day, and I'm tempted to log out and check for her, but if I do that now, I won't look good. And then I won't be able to help either of us.

I exit the house and kill two dying Common Ghouls with my new Granite Hatchet (yes, it's made from those Granite Bricks, Plant Twine, and Common Sticks) which kills them in five hits instead of six. A slight improvement. I don't bother with the mob drops and check the area for Lavaworms. I spot one bouncing away in the distance only to stop next to a wandering Duck. The monster doesn't spray the peaceful mob with fire and lava. I'm jealous.

But remembering the Lava Incident gives me an idea.

"Time to graduate to the second grade," I say. "It's experiment time."

I need to bring the Dreadmoths to me. Days upon days of watching my dirt tower, water trap has confirmed that Dreadmoths don't spawn in enclosed spaces. And I already know from the Lava Incident that they're attracted to light. I doubt that's changed in the update. They're moths. I've seen enough of them in real life swarming street lamps to know Salvos won't change that part of their behavior.

But before I build a trap, I need to get into the sky.

More like, I need to finally reach the top of that cliff.

* * * * *

Ladders are easy to make, at least. I get two by placing two columns of Common Sticks around a column of Plant Twines. It's a bit time consuming to gather the materials, but worth it, because I'm able to just stick the ladder pieces, each of which is half my height, to the side of the cliff. They stay on as if I've crazy glued them.

And they stay on as I haul myself up them. I don't tire during the climb, at least, and I can let go with one hand and tap my inventory with the other, summoning a weapon, tool, or item into my hand. This allows me to stick ladder after ladder just above me, climb a bit more, and repeat. It doesn't obey the laws of physics but neither does most of Salvosera. But I like the charm.

"Just don't look down, Mike," I mutter.

So of course, I do.

"Look back up, or you *will* need an adult diaper," I say, dizzy. The ground is at least fifty feet below at me at this point, and I'm only two-thirds of the way up this cliff. My heart pounds as I forget I'm in a game for a moment. But my footing is good and feels stable, more stable than it would in real life. I can imagine Fatigue would make climbing difficult and more realistic, but I'm fine for now.

And at long, long last, I reach the top of that tall cliff.

Hauling myself up onto the grass is easy, but as soon as I do, dizziness comes over me as I stare at the sprawling Scattered Woods below. I can see my house and—yikes—a single Lavaworm that's been camping on my roof. I'll need to light it because I'm lucky it didn't ambush me when I exited my house this morning. I'm also looking down on the top of my waterfall-fed barley farm and the dirt tower that houses my water trap. My tree farm is a thick row of neat growth and I can even see foggy hints of my Swamp Ghoul grinder from here. A small hole near it reveals my Peat mine which I've been working on for some time.

Then dread comes over me. I've got to back away from the edge of the cliff, because a fall like this will kill me. When I do, I lose track of the ladder.

Then another thought hits me.

"I'm going to have to climb back down eventually." Or slowly dig a staircase down with my new Granite Hammer. I back over short, bright green grass, breathing in chilly air. I sigh in relief and stop near another tree.

Is that a patch of snow over there?

It's cold up here. The small snow patch feels like the real thing when I lean down and press my hand into it. I don't leave a print or anything, but it's interesting and just adds to the weird charm. Hopefully Dreadmoths don't have an aversion to cold or my newest trap isn't going to work. They shouldn't. They spawn at this height all the time. I first eye the cliff. It's a narrow, flat surface for the most part with a couple of trees, but it extends lengthwise as far as I can see. And the cliff is thinner than I thought. From my position, I can even see the Flatlands biome I visited, plus the pool of lava in the distance, partially obscured by fog.

"Are you kidding?" I shout at the sky. "That pool of lava was *this* close to my base?"

All that time I was messing with molds and clay buckets, I was less than fifty meters from my house. Balling my fists, I count my paces across the top of the cliff. Yes. The cliff is just fifty meters wide but hundreds long. I could have dug through it with my hammer and saved a buttload of time.

I force myself to calm down. "That's a project for another time," I say, eyeing the sky. The clouds seem closer now. I must be at least forty blocks in the air, judging from the ladders I made. If I light up the top of this cliff, I should stop ground mobs from spawning and leave more room for Dreadmoths. Being higher up might also cut the spawn rate in that massive cave, further helping me lure in more of what I want. I haven't done any studies to find out for sure, but that's just what I've seen.

I tap my backpack to open my inventory. I have blocks. Lots of Common Planks, which stack to 99 in each slot. More Ladders. About thirty ~~Crap~~ Peat Torches because I've used up all my Spark Clusters, and haven't gotten more from my trap so far. Dreadmoths like light. The Lava Incident proved that.

And then I need to kill them and collect the bounty.

And after that, I'll have a full set of armor.

And after that, I'm showing Salvos what Mike Wattles is all about.

CHAPTER TWENTY-SIX

"And this, ladies and gentlemen, is the Mike Wattles Dreadmoth Destroyer."

My Dreadmoth Destroyer is on a Common Plank column another thirty meters or so above the top of the cliff. At least the build height in Salvosera is high enough for me to do this. I'd been worrying about that.

I stand in the middle of my creation and explain the logic of my newest invention. "I've got a ladder going to the top of this tower and I enter the wooden structure through the floor. You can see a trapdoor there." I motion to the middle of the tower's floor, where a dark trapdoor waits. "And my octagon tower, I know, is blasphemy in a world of pentagons."

It's fancier than my house, sadly. And brighter. Windows on every side and one Peat Torch above each window keep things lit. Turns out I can only place Peat Torches on non-transparent things, but that's fine. I can see what I'll be doing.

"Maybe I'm not such a bad builder. This thing looks like a wooden version of that tower in Canada," I say. "These windows let me see what I'm doing and I can bravely hack at the Dreadmoths from in here." I've got Common Slabs above each window, leaving a hole for me to use.

But it's *really* cold up here and the air is thin. And having openings doesn't help.

I shiver. "At least my irrigated Fertile Farmland blocks don't freeze. That was another thing I was worried over." I walk to the windows and look down at the outer part of my tower. A wooden platform surrounds it on all sides, and a wooden wall on the other side of that platform blocks my view of the world.

I turn my gaze down at the water streams I've got flowing from the four irrigated farmland blocks, one on each "corner" of my tower. Water flows ten blocks from each source, in each direction, to two collection channels that lead inside.

"This running water noise won't make me have to go to the bathroom," I say. But at least 1.) I won't die in my murder hole and 2.) Only Dreadmoths should spawn up here, and my distance from that massive cave should cut down on underground monster spawns and increase the spawns up here.

"So basically, the Dreadmoths will fly towards the light down here and sink between the inner and outer walls of my tower. Then I'll kill them and let the water bring their plates to me. The walls will stop their drops from falling to the ground."

The light outside dims. Then the sky goes dark and only the pale light from the Peat Torches outside filters through the windows.

My theory that being up here, way off the ground, will make more Dreadmoths spawn turns out to be right.

I hear screeches, some fairly close, some far away.

"Yes," I hiss, readying my Granite Hatchet. I swing it, relishing the whooshing noise it makes. It's a much more satisfying sound than the one the Flint Hatchet made.

And then I wait, hoping that the Peat Torches do their thing.

But halfway through the night, I realize that I named Peat Torches *Crap Torches* for a reason. Towards the end of the night, one Dreadmoth wanders close to my tower, and then dives in between the walls and into my kill range as it emits an ear-splitting screech.

I swing and make the kill quickly, without taking any damage, and finally a coveted Dreadmoth Plate falls into my water stream and slowly makes its way, along with some Silk, to one of my collection points. The Plate and Silk ride into my tower under another Common Slab I've got up for safety and settle on the floor.

The sun's coming back up. Pink light invades my windows.

I pick up my prize.

"One Dreadmoth."

I eye my inventory. A whole night's earned me this prize. In a week, I might have enough for a chestplate. And that's if I'm lucky.

A mirthless laugh rises in my throat. "I've got to do better."

Of course, first tries on these mob traps rarely work well. I'm guessing that light sources are a tiered thing like Ovens and tools. Or I simply need more weaker light sources to attract more Dreadmoths. Lava attracted that one Dreadmoth with no issue, so it must be considered a strong light source, and I imagine that Spark Clusters can make something with brightness between the Peat Torches and Lava.

But the problem is that my tower is wood.

Spark Clusters it is.

But to get Spark Clusters, I'll need to make another extremely risky cave run without armor. And *that's* a great idea.

"What to do, Mike?" I pace around the Dreadmoth Destroyer as the remaining Dreadmoths despawn, one by one, in the daylight. The screeches vanish. Lava's not an option. I could rebuild this whole thing with dirt so I could use lava, maybe put it inside a glass tower, but I still suspect Salvos has made lava burn through Clay Pails. "Okay," I say, thinking out loud. "The safest option is to add more Crap Torches. Lots of them. I can go back to the Peat mine. Make a staircase tunnel down and see if I can find some Spark Ore down there too. Worst case, I just end up with a lot of Peat." Then I think of Anthony Anton and add, "Testing is just part of the business." He should know that. And besides, I'm still alive and making progress.

I climb down from the tower, throwing open the trapdoor I've placed over the exit. Dizziness comes over me as I eye the top of the cliff way below. Yikes. But I gulp and lower myself down the ladder, rung by rung, descending faster than I would in real life. Then once I set my shivering legs down on the grass of the cliff, I sigh, walk over to the two Common Plank columns I've placed to mark the location of my second ladder, and descend that one as well.

It's late morning by the time I make it down to my house. No Lavaworms wander around today which is strange, but then I remember that being so far in the air stopped mobs from spawning on the ground. I find none in the dirt tower trap, either. Bummer.

I walk over to the border of the Northern Swamp. A few Swamp Ghouls wander out of my first trap and try to traverse the Glass Panes, only to die in the sun as they're slowed by the Leaves. I ignore them and walk over to my Peat mine. It's still there, ten blocks deep now, stopping partway under the lake where I first saw Swamp Ghouls. I've left a single burning Peat Torch on the wall in there to prevent mob spawns and it seems to have worked, though I can barely see the end of the short tunnel. At least they don't go out, because I placed that torch sometime last week.

A strange wave of nostalgia sweeps over me. I spent my first night out here, looking at those dead trees out on the lake and the mysterious green light I still haven't figured out. But the sun's already approaching noon so I need to get to work.

"This had better be productive." I walk into the tunnel. Dark Peat surrounds me on all sides and makes up the floor, and Damp Soil makes up the ceiling. The whole place smells the way I'd expect a swamp would. The embers of the Peat Torch brighten a bit as I pass and cast a breeze on it—a cool effect that wasn't in 1.0, I've got to admit— and dim again. After moving my Granite Shovel and Granite Hammer to my hotbar, I get to work tunneling not only forward, but downward, keeping my tunnel three polygons wide. Globs of Peat drop and I pull them into my inventory, and I realize the light's so dim I can't tell what I'm doing anymore. I add my last Peat Torch into my hotbar, which appears in my hand, but before I can place it, the ground falls out from under me and I'm falling through a void.

I find myself standing in the Salvos Simulator a moment later, whirling to face whoever logged me out. I wasn't in the game for that long, was I? Still, I'm not shocked to see Candi standing there, one lock of red hair hanging over the front of her suit. She's balancing her laptop on her hip and forcing a smile at me so hard that I wonder what disaster is about to befall me now.

CHAPTER TWENTY-SEVEN

"You log me out a lot." That's all I can mutter as I take off my helmet and then the gloves. I almost slip on the floor of the Simulator.

"I log everybody out a lot," Candi says as her grin drops off.

Ouch. I'm tired of these mixed signals. "Was I about to screw up on something?"

But then she waves me out, erasing every indication that yes, I was about to screw up. "You all have been working hard. We're going to Dill and Steve's tonight. All of us."

"Dill and Steve's?" I ask as she backs away. Behind her, Don stands, removing his own helmet. He's broken a sweat and lets out a breath. Has he died since 1.1 started? I can't tell. And behind him, Val climbs out of her own Simulator, pulling her haptic gloves off. We've got a full house tonight. All of us have come down to the testing room.

"Yeah. The adult arcade. You've never been there?" Candi asks. "You're the only local guy. Mondays are by far the best days to go. The place is a lot less busy."

"We go out together once in a while," Don says, catching me up.

"Of course I know what Dill and Steve's is. Natalie and I went there on her birthday two years ago with some friends of hers," I say, hating that I'm giving off sour grapes.

Candi frowns. "Yeah. We all need to take a break. I know 1.1 is different, but I have instructions from the top that our gamers need to avoid burnout." She stares at the wall as she speaks and I somehow doubt that's the truth.

"No kidding," Val says, pulling her braids back.

Apparently everyone's been adjusting. I feel less stupid but no less rejected.

Despite making a bit of progress and not dying in Salvosera, my mood plunges into the toilet as I wait my turn to get changed. Once everyone's out of the changing room, Candi waves us to the underground garage. Even the thought of having a fun night at Dill and Steve's doesn't lift my mood that much.

We cram into a pair of cars to take the drive to the arcade. It's not that packed on a Monday night which I'm sure is why Candi chose today to take us all out. She drives the car I share with Don and Val while Kevin, Liz, and Matt take the other car. I wonder if any of them have died in-game and will come back to eviction notices.

Candi checks us all in to Dill and Steve's at the front counter using Anton's credit card. The woman at the front desk gawks at it before swiping. A lot of people must know who Anton is. Creationist. Duh. He's only the most famous VR developer in the world.

"Everyone has five hundred credits. We meet for dinner in the restaurant in two hours," Candi says, motioning to the huge arcade floor and the attached burger joint. She seems so carefree right now but I can't help but wonder if she's got a motive for logging all of us out at the same time. Candi might have zero interest in me but I've got to look for any warning signals.

And I've got to mention Natalie. I promised her that.

I pair up with Matt for the next couple of hours, trying to enjoy myself. We play a few racing games, a couple of first person shooters, and that one game where you cut fruit on a touch screen. I'm not great at any of them. Unlike Val and Kevin, I'm not big into actual combat or reflexes. But I have fun all the same, and I take a while to realize that Candi's been pretty absent during the past couple of hours.

"Doesn't Candi ever hang out with us?" I ask once we finish a round of the corny fruit game.

Matt shrugs. "Not really. I mean, she's around, but she's not really around. I think aloof is the word. She reminds me of a cat."

"Good comparison," I grumble.

"Come on. She's so busy she couldn't date anyone if she wanted." Matt slaps me on the back. "Don't take it personally. I don't think any of us have dated within our group. It would ruin things, you know?"

"Gotta love that drama," I say. I can't bear to tell him that Beta 1.1 could ruin things and not just on the gaming front. But I have the feeling Matt's pretty safe. He's got that big subscriber base he can bring to Salvosera thanks to his long walk to the Glitch Lands. Kevin and Val are both straight-up PVP and Liz is more of an explorer who hunts down new features. If Salvos wants to make cuts, they won't need two PVP people. And explorers can only do so much.

And then there's me.

I'm here because Miriam went over Anton's head.

"Say, it's almost dinner." Matt peels himself from the fruit game and motions to the burger joint. "There's Candi."

Despite the vibes she's been sending me I look forward to it. We all sit at the same table and joke around like old friends and I can see why dating is a no go. We're just a group of nerdy gamers. Friends. Comrades. Maybe even a family. We order greasy burgers with butter buns and fries that come with a whole tray of weird sauces. I'm careful not to partake in the booze on the menu, despite there being a ton of drinks with ridiculous names like *Dancing With A Moose* and *Beach Combing In Underwear*. I'm the only one who doesn't order a beer with the other guys, and as the time creeps toward ten PM, Matt and Don get up and stretch.

"So," Candi says, pocketing her phone. "How is everyone doing?"

"Great," Matt says.

"Having fun," Kevin adds.

"Finally got done lighting up that cave," Liz adds.

Everyone offers vague answers, following the non-disclosure rule.

"Fine," I say.

Candi nods. "Glad to see that everyone's enjoying 1.1 so far. I know there are some new and surprise features."

Val nods but says nothing.

"Peat sucks," I blurt.

Candi snaps her gaze to me. Have I said too much? I snap my mouth shut, but Candi smiles. "Don't worry. We all know so you're not spoiling any secrets. So, Crap Torches is your nickname for those."

I must have muttered it to myself more than once while trying to light up that one cavern and maybe again while making my Dreadmoth Destroyer.

"Um, yes," I say as everyone laughs.

"My nickname for them is far worse," Candi says. "Just take a synonym for 'crap' and you have what I mean."

More laughter sounds. But Candi doesn't join in.

"It's best to move on to something better as soon as possible, as you've found out," Candi says. "Peat mines are no good. Fast, but not worth it." Then she clams up as her cheeks pale and her gaze flicks to her pants pocket where the phone is located. Awesome. It's got to be bugged. If anyone can screw with technology, it's the government or Anthony Anton.

Candi is trapped beyond belief.

No one says anything about it. No one's dumb enough to comment on it. It's a silent understanding.

Candi wipes her mouth. "We've got three more hours until the place closes." She rises. "I'm going to get some fresh air and come back in. Maybe I'll join you at the claw machine in a bit."

I watch as she empties her tray and heads to the front doors. Matt looks at me, eyes full of shock, letting me know I'm about to miss a super obvious cue. Even if Candi's not interested in dating any of us, she knows more than what she's letting on, and besides, I still have to let her know to check out Natalie's channel.

So I follow, and no one says a word.

The line out front has emptied but I'm still wearing my plastic armband to get back in. I find Candi leaning against the building and staring at the expressway on ramp a quarter mile away. The sounds of light traffic fill the night.

"Hey," I say, not sure whether I should approach.

She motions me over. "Having fun?" A warning to watch every word lurks between her words. Yes. She wants to talk to me as much as she's allowed.

The rest just might be a ruse.

"Yeah. This is great," I say.

"I'm sorry I couldn't make it to Natalie's weekend thing. I got your note and your sister sounds cool," Candi says. "I wanted to show up but I'm just so busy. I've been playing Creationist forever and that, combined with this, is catching up to me."

"That sucks," I say, joining her in leaning against the building. "Can't you take a break?" Who is Candi, really? How did she get involved with Salvos Corporation?

"Not during this time. It wasn't so bad in alpha, when it was just me doing the testing," she says. "Then I got to handle all the rest. They told me I'm good at putting things together. That I can relate to other gamers." She rolls her eyes and looks at the sky, and I sense the massive strain she's under. But she says nothing more.

The bulge of the phone is still lurking in her pocket.

We're pushing our boundaries. "Work can catch up with you. I'm glad we can have nights out." I clear my throat and Candi looks to me. "Say, if you need any more players, even in the future, my sister Natalie is awesome at playing arena maps and hardcore survival. You should have seen her playing one of Vox's maps the other night. The Barrens."

"Oh. That one," Candi says with a smile. "Tough map. Just surviving to the end is an accomplishment."

"Ever played that one?"

"Several times," she says. "What's your sister's player name?"

Natalie might have a chance. It's a start. "ElfQueen546. Her skin is, well, an elf queen. And that's her GameTube channel name, too. Even if you can just get her more subs, that would be helpful."

Candi nods. "I'll see what I can do. I can imagine she's tough, like you."

"Um..."

Compliment.

Yeah.

"Thanks. You don't know what this means," I say. Maybe, if I do somehow screw up and get killed, Natalie will be able to come in and earn some money for herself. "I'm not trying to create trouble or anything, so I get it if you can't." *I'm sorry,* is what I want to say.

Candi's eyes sparkle. Is she amused? Why? I did nothing but put pressure on her. This was a fight I never wanted, but one I have to have. Thanks, desperation. But maybe Salvos is making her miserable and she's glad I'm being a thorn in its side. A man can hope.

"I'll do my best," she says. "Salvos might decide it's about to have openings soon. You never know. People make mistakes all the time, especially when it comes to caves and cliffs." She stares at me, deadly serious again, before she peels herself from the wall to head back inside. "Come on. The claw machine's waiting, and we're getting that stuffed turtle I saw in there earlier."

CHAPTER TWENTY-EIGHT

One of my reports showed up in the break room yesterday.

Natalie's buzzing text wakes me early the next morning and that's what I find when I grab my phone. Huh? I blink, remembering how late we were all out last night. But I read the text again, trying to understand.

A report? I text.

Yes. About company spending. They're confidential. I swear, I didn't leave it there.

I swallow. Natalie's told me about them before, spreadsheets she has to do about spending for her boss, and they're not supposed to be anyone else's knowledge. If one of them got left in the break room—

I gulp. *Did anyone find out?*

Kristen told me about it this morning. The cleaning lady slid it under Mark's door with a note.

Kristen is a co-worker that has an office next to Natalie's. I gulp. Her boss, Mark, can't can her for short-term disability, but the law doesn't stop him from canning her for some other reason. I shoot out of bed, pacing as I text. Natalie couldn't have completed the process for filing for disability yet, and if she has, it won't matter if something like this blows up. *Does he have a key to your cabinet?*

She doesn't answer for a bit. I open the fridge and stare at the leftover pizza boxes, then slam it again.

I shouldn't have printed it. But the stupid program corrupted the file last time.

I ball my fists at the injustice of it all. Clearly her boss has lured her into a trap and maybe even planted that report himself. Now he has a reason to worm out of paying disability. Mark should work for Salvos Corporation. Wow, I can't believe I'm thinking that.

Lawyer. NOW. Before he does a meeting. I text her a link with a bunch of local lawyers and make a couple of recommendations. I hate throwing this on her when she's already sick and struggling, but what else can I do? *Any cameras at your work?*

Don't think so. But thanks. I will. Taking a half day for an appointment anyway.

And thanks for that first payment!

She's gone after that. Yes. Mark's been setting her up forever, building a record, making his case. I want to kill him. But I let out a breath and change my clothes. The best thing I can do for Natalie is make sure I stay alive in Salvosera. She needs to know she can lean on me.

Thumps from down the hall jar me. Angry shouts follow.

What is going on out there?

I open my apartment door. Down the hall, near the elevator door, Val's apartment door is standing open and sliding noises are coming from inside.

"What—?" I start.

"I can't believe this," Val says, furious, from two doors down the hall. "This wasn't in the contract. I did *not* terminate my own testing period."

I gulp.

Last night, Candi mentioned mistakes made in caves and on cliffs, and the fact that Salvos might have openings soon. And I understand: last night, Val was about to die in a cave or about to fall to her death.

Candi logged us out right before it happened, maybe to give her a chance to think about how to save herself.

But it didn't work.

"We're sorry. The contract clearly states that the conditions for termination can change," a man says in her apartment.

"I saw that, but don't we have to be notified?" Val asks.

I storm out of my apartment. Did Salvos pull a trick on her? I march right to her door which is cracked an inch.

"What's going on in here?" I ask, knowing full well I shouldn't get involved. But Val, PrincessKitty21, is my friend. She's not facing this alone.

I find Val standing over a bunch of folded cardboard boxes that have been thrown at her feet. She's got her arms crossed over her hot pink shirt and she's staring up at two guys in suits I've never seen. Neither guy appears intimidated. An older man with a no-nonsense look in his eyes holds paperwork. He's the one who turns to me and narrows his eyes.

"This is not your business," he says in a patient tone that infuriates me.

Yes, it is. "Why are you kicking her out? She did nothing wrong!"

"Close the door," the older man snaps at his partner, a younger one. It's clear that leaving it open was an error.

But I put my foot between the door and the frame, and the young guy looks like he doesn't want to chance it. "No. What are you doing to her?"

Val's eyes widen in warning. She knows about Natalie. While I've stayed shut up about my pay, I mentioned moving her into my apartment if things get bad. And I'm putting myself and my sister in danger.

What am I doing? Dad would have a panic attack.

"Young man," the older one says, pushing up his glasses. "Your contracts have provisions for changing the conditions of your residence here and ability to participate in the closed beta program. Though I am Salvos Corporation's Regional Manager, I am not at liberty to explain the exact changing terms. But they are done in the best interest of all parties."

This is one hundred percent a threat. I'm not proud of it, but I take my foot from the door and back up a bit. I don't realize why at first, but then Val walks over to me, stare warning me not to aggro these guys any further.

She takes a breath, calming herself. "Mike. It'll be fine. I'll be okay. I'm just a tiny bit annoyed right now," she says, choosing her words carefully. "I've got somewhere I can go and a fan base that'll keep me going. We'll still play Creationist online together. I'll stay in contact with all of you."

"You sure?" I know she can't say anything with these guys here, or even after she leaves, or even on a private Creationist server, thanks to that non-disclosure agreement. The guys' stern faces tell me she'd better not say a word.

"Positive," she says, lifting her tone and opening her arms for a hug.

I shove my anger down and we hug. "Good luck out there, Val."

Then we separate and she stares at me, all serious. "It was fun. We'll play together again once Salvosera starts multiplayer. All of us." Then she turns to the two guys. "Are either of you going to help me pack, at least? Because if you don't, I'll have Mike help me."

The trap works, and I grin as the two guys assemble the flattened cardboard boxes. They don't want me and Val alone in the same apartment where we could speak freely, even if the place is bugged. Val doesn't have much in her apartment but enough to give the old Regional Manager a backache when he's done. And that I'm glad for.

* * * * *

Are my chances better now that our group has been whittled down to six?

Yes, I decide. My chances are twice as good as they were. And I feel like a jerk for the thought because that means Val's gone. But I want to find Candi to make sure she meant Val when she was talking about an opening. And I want to remind her to check out Natalie's channel.

Give it up, a voice says in my head as I get off the elevator and walk into the testing room. Two people are already suited up and immersed, probably Matt and Liz. They're still here. But what about Candi?

She got me in here. She knew I needed help and that's a big part of the reason why I'm here.

I don't find her in the lounge, either, or the meeting room. The rest of the place seems empty today. I think of going up to her apartment which is on the floor above mine, but I talk myself out of it before I can get up the nerve. What gives? I know Candi secretly hates this arrangement and we have to stick together. But the more I'm around her, the less I believe I'm ever going to figure her out.

CHAPTER TWENTY-NINE

I can't let all these thoughts torment me. Salvosera waits and it's still my biggest shot at helping Natalie once per boss fully puts together his screwed-up case against her. I don't know what else to do. I'm not a lawyer and don't know every aspect of law but I sense a lengthy legal battle before Natalie, one that she's not going to have the energy to face.

And she won't be able to deal with it if she's on the streets, like I might be if I don't make sure I make progress and stay alive.

So with a heavy heart, I head back to the testing room. Liz waves to me as she emerges from the changing room.

"Hey," she says. Then she must see my long face because she approaches, helmet under her arm. "What's up?"

"Val's being made to leave," I say, not caring about the cameras.

Liz's eyes widen. "She's what?"

I am taking another massive risk. "I don't know what their reasoning is but she's moving out. She told me she'd be okay." *Don't die, Liz. Please.* I don't want to see any of us get kicked out of here, but I know that one more of us will have to go. We're the herd. Anthony said so himself. And now he's got us racing against each other, scrambling for a prize.

"What? I have to go up and say goodbye to her," Liz says, eyeing the elevator.

"No," I say, moving to block her. And I hate that I'm doing it. Salvos won't like it if we all go up and put attention on the spectacle the Regional Manager didn't want me to see. What am I becoming? I'm just parroting them so I can avoid being the next one taking a trip into the wood chipper, and I hate it. Maybe Candi and I have more in common than I think.

"Why are you stopping me?" Liz asks. "Val's my friend."

I fumble for an excuse. "You can't leave the testing room in your Salvos Suit." I haven't seen too many other people in this apartment building but I'm sure Salvos wouldn't like us parading around in our futuristic gear.

"Geez, Mike. Quit being such a stickler for the rules. Well behaved women never make history." Liz huffs but she backs off, waiting for her turn in the changing room...again. Don emerges in his suit and looks after Liz, confused. He's also holding his black helmet under his arm.

She's right. I'm so worried about getting kicked out that I'm acting like a puppet, and I hate it. Don looks at me, still confused.

"It's nothing," I say, hating myself.

But Natalie—

I have to hold on for her.

She comes first.

"Liz's upset. I might be a guy, but I know when something's wrong," Don says.

I gulp. Can this get any worse? I eye the cameras on the ceiling and the elevator door, but no goons come in to escort me off the premises. Maybe I haven't broken any rules.

"Val's packing up her apartment." I leave it at that.

Don's eyes widen. "What? She was fine last night."

I don't want to try to convince anyone anymore. "I don't know what it was about. I think she's still here, though. She told me goodbye." Stupid camera. If we were off the premises, I might be able to open up to Don, but Salvos would probably find a way to track that, too.

Liz emerges from the changing room, back in her plaid and jeans, and rushes upstairs. Don dives into the changing room to get back in his everyday clothes, and once he's done, that leaves me with Matt and Kevin, who are both immersed in their games. Neither of the figures can be Candi. She's missing in action right now.

I wonder how she's holding up.

But, Natalie.

I should let Matt and Liz say their goodbyes to Val. I don't know how to log out Kevin and Don, so there's nothing I can do at the moment since Candi seems to hold the controls for that. If it's possible for us to do, Matt and Liz would have done it. And Candi must already know about Val and she's not logging them out, either.

So what I have to do next is clear.

Contract conditions can change at any time. That must be in the missing pages of mine, among other horrible things. I've got to get into Salvosera and keep wowing corporate.

So I dive into the changing room, find my suit, stuff my clothes in my locker, and get into the closest empty box. I shove all the uncomfortable thoughts from my mind. They won't help me now. The blue light bathes me as the plastic pads tingle against the bare skin of my chest, arms, and thighs. My helmet goes completely dark inside, and with a wave of dizziness and a falling sensation, I'm logging in.

I blink, and the dull light of the peat mine greets me. I'm standing near the end of my tunnel, and I remember that I've made a staircase down with my Granite Hammer and Shovel. The dank smell of peat and swamp surrounds me again. I blink, getting my bearings. I've tunneled in far enough so that I can't see the outside and I've collected some Clumps of Peat. A stack of ninety-nine rests in my hotbar and I move it into my inventory. That should be enough to make a ton of Crap Torches and maybe enough to attract more Dreadmoths. But Spark Ore would be better. While I'm here, I should make a staircase down into the Common Stone layer and do some boring strip mining. The key will be to light my way as I go.

At least I've reached stone, having cleared all the Peat from the floor. I keep my hotbar in my view and tap my Crap Torches, highlighting the wooden box. A torch appears in my hand, glowing with embers, and I highlight the Peat wall to place it. Better. Weak light floods the area and I can see.

I equip my Granite Hammer and continue my dig.

Until, five seconds later, a crackling noise erupts behind me.

I jump, heart leaping into my throat, and whirl, swinging my Hammer at the Lavaworm behind me. But there's no Lavaworm. I swing through empty air as I backpedal into the end of the tunnel. I grunt. Now I can see my tunnel entrance, fifty feet away. The last of the daylight is fading, but no monsters have come into the tunnel with me.

The crackling sound stays. And it's close.

What the heck?

The wall.

I gulp before I register what's happening.

Um, Mike?

Peat. Is flammable.

The wall holding the newly-placed torch is on fire. The dark Peat has turned an animated orange and now gives off small fire particles. The Crap Torch pops off the wall and vanishes into a puff of smoke, but the wall stays lit, and then the flames spread to the next block, and the next.

"What?" The first torch didn't do this. It's still on the wall near the tunnel's entrance, twenty meters away, but then as I watch, it, too, sets its wall on fire. "What the heck?"

The update.

Peat wasn't like this before. And when I placed the second torch, the first one updated with the new mechanics and said, *hey, this needs to screw up Mike Wattles's day.*

"Mike, do something!" I switch to my Shovel and dig out the burning Peat, but it drops nothing and now I've got three more burning chunks of it to deal with. No, four. And that doesn't count the burning stuff near the entrance. The air clouds as it fills with transparent, grayish blocks. The tunnel reeks of smoke. My eyes water.

My status bars shoot up into my vision, and the one I've never used before—the one on the lower right with the air bubbles and the blue bar—begins to deplete, slowly at first, but then it drops faster and faster and approaches half.

Oxygen.

Get out.

I cough as my tears flow. I stumble up the steps, instinct taking over. My vision blurs as a pair of debuffs appear in the top right of my view—the shaking hand of Fatigue and a black cloud.

Through my blurry vision, I can see that the burning Peat has spread to parts of the ceiling and even the opposite wall. This fire spread is no joke. Hostility level of 70 or not, I've got better chances outside.

"Good thing I didn't block this tunnel!" I run to the exit, stumbling and weak as I switch back to my Granite Hammer, the best weapon I've got against Swamp Ghouls. I emerge into the dark, breathing in clean air, though smoke globs emerge behind me and rise into the sky. The crackling stays intense but my Oxygen rises quickly as I gasp, and the debuffs blink and vanish. My vision clears and my strength comes back.

It was a trap.

Anton knew I would have to go back into that Peat tunnel.

They made the area slow to update on purpose. He *knew* I would trigger a peat fire.

I hold a rude hand gesture in the air as I start my run to my distant base. For all he knows, I'm flipping off the fire.

But more Swamp Ghouls *sclorc* at me and I realize I'm next to my Swamp Ghoul grinder.

And at night, the Slaughter Chute doesn't kill them.

About a dozen leftover spawns from the daytime are alive and well, pushing through the Common Leaves. And the first five have already freed themselves, blocking the way back to my base. They lumber towards me, arms extended.

"Uh," I mutter.

I back off, listening to the sounds of more Ghouls behind me, splashing their way closer through the lake.

A quick assessment tells me my chances of surviving a fight with them all is close to zero.

Wait.

My cave.

My crappy first night shelter is right next to me. And I've got plenty of blocks with me to barricade myself.

I dodge a Ghoul and dive in, pulling the chunks of Common Stone into my hotbar as the Swamp Ghoul mob closes in. At least they won't dig through that. I leave a small window so I can hack at them while I catch my breath.

Mistakes can be made in caves.

Peat mines are no good.

"Mike, you're an idiot." Candi was trying to warn me about the dangers of Peat and I didn't notice.

I can see the entrance to the Peat mine from here, and it's glowing like a tunnel to a fiery underworld. Smoke continues to billow out and rise into the sky. It's showing no signs of stopping. Every chunk of Peat must be on fire in the there by now. I barely got out in time.

And maybe the Peat fire is spreading under the ground, too.

Small smoke particles rise from the soild ground above the mine and even from the part of the lake the mine goes under. It's not a small fire.

I swing at two Swamp Ghouls through the small hole I've left at the cave entrance. I kill them in five hits each, leaving my view free again. I lean out a bit. Once again, something's off.

Are the smoke particles spreading?

I gulp.

Yep. The area giving them off is growing by the second, spreading through the swamp. So Peat fires don't need open air to burn. And the cave is still a blast furnace.

Soon, the whole swamp will be on fire under the Damp Soil.

"Unbelievable!"

But maybe it won't be a big deal. A couple more Swamp Ghouls are walking on top of the ground, unharmed, so it seems the small smoke particles are cosmetic only. I let out a breath and a sigh of relief. So far, I've only found Peat in the Northern Swamp. The fire should stay here. Maybe it will even make my Swamp Ghoul grinder more efficient if it lights up the underground.

"I can live with this," I mutter, watching as the smoke particles spread to the mouth of my cave and then to the very edge of the Northern Swamp biome, where my grinder is set up. The air doesn't even heat, though it smells faintly of smoke. Under my feet is a raging inferno, one I can faintly hear crackling, but so long as I've got stone and dirt between me and it, I should be good.

I lean against the wall, watching the stars slowly rise. As I listen, the Swamp Ghoul mob slowly disperses since they can't find a way to me, probably. "Mike, that was close. Today you learned."

And then another orange flash catches my attention from my right.

I turn and dare to peek my head out the small opening I've left.

A Common Tree at the edge of the biome border has caught fire at the base, and the flames spread up the tree and consume its leaves, giving off more smoke. A few seconds later, the next tree catches fire, and the next...

I gulp.

Peat fires spread to nearby wood.

The Scattered Forest is catching fire.

And I've replanted a lot of trees since starting my game. There's so much tinder, so much flammable material between me and—

I raise my Hammer. "My base!"

CHAPTER THIRTY

Without my base, not only will my chances of death rise by about two hundred percent, but Salvos would find a reason to get rid of me. The special conditions in the contract's missing pages must have a clause about what happens if your base gets destroyed.

If it doesn't, why would Anton add peat fires to the game?

Logic propels me to bash the Common Stone barrier with my Hammer. My mind works. Fires will light the area and stop most hostile mob spawns. Maybe. Once I've got a two-meter high hole in the barrier, I bolt out, Hammer still equipped, and I run for it.

The crackling sound seems to be everywhere. Already five trees near the edge of the Northern Swamp have caught fire, and a Swamp Ghoul does the same as it stupidly wanders too close to the trees. Then it spots me, forgets that it's on fire and taking constant damage, and makes a beeline in my direction.

Fine. I swing my hammer and strike it in the chest, throwing it back and watching it die. In the distance, faint light from my wooden house, wooden ladder, and wooden Dreadmoth Destroyer shines through the still-living trees.

Stopping the fire from here will be impossible. Already two more trees go up, lit by the ones already on fire. And nothing's going out. Why did I have to plant so many trees around my base? Bad idea, and probably something else Anton noticed. The whole area could be burning by daybreak, which takes place in maybe twenty minutes.

My best hope is clearing all the trees near my base. I've got to take the most dangerous run in the dark I've ever taken.

I run.

Hammer raised, I swing at a Common Ghoul, throwing it out of the way. I gasp for breath, breathing in the smoke that rides on the wind. Crap. The wind is blowing from the fire *towards* my base. The crackling gets fainter behind me as the world turns dark. More Ghouls make *sclorc* sounds somewhere to the left. My sides hurt as I dodge trees. I lose sight of my base and remember that I'm near my thick tree farm, where I planted rows of trees just a three blocks apart each.

It's gonna go up within ten minutes.

And then it's going to leap to my base, which has another dozen trees between the farm and it.

"Go, go, go!" Equipping my Granite Hatchet, I get to work in the dark, listening to the clunking sound of cutting wood. Sweat breaks out on my palms. My arms strain with the effort. I cut down the first tree, the second...and then the faint sound of something hopping on grass approaches from behind.

No. *Not now.*

Fire spread is out of control now...and there's a Lavaworm right behind me.

I whirl, raising my Hatchet, and I swing at the faintly glowing, grimacing coil. I strike it right in the face as it starts to crackle, and it flies back enough to knock it off. Then I lunge forward and strike again, but the monster hits another tree that's not part of my farm and brightens as it gets ready to erupt.

"There she blows!" I back off as it bursts into polygons of lava, ember particles, and falling flames, which ignite the grass and spread to the tree. "Please, Salvosera gods. Don't make Lavaworms that destructive."

Light fills my tiny part of the night as the tree burns a bit, but this fire doesn't spread like the peat fire does. The first bit of fire dies and while lava spreads on the ground, sizzling, I back off. I'm alive. Undamaged. At least Lavaworm fire has some sort of cap on its duration.

But the faint glow of the approaching peat inferno sure doesn't seem to. Through the trees, a distant orange glow slowly gets brighter. My heart races and I'm sure I'll never clear enough forest in time to stop it from reaching my base. Leaves take forever to decay and they'll go up no problem.

"I need a Plan B," I mutter, backing towards my base, which must be in the opposite direction as the glow.

The screech of a Dreadmoth sounds in the direction of the fire. One of the creatures is approaching, drawn by the glow of the flames.

A horrific screech fills the air as I look up to see the outline of a giant moth against the stars. A green ball sails at me—from at least twenty blocks away—and I dodge to the side as it lands near the patch of now-drying lava. A hissing sound rises as they meet, but I don't stay to look at the end result. I clear another couple of trees and see my base, bright compared to the night. I'll never hit the Dreadmoth from here and I don't have time to fight it, especially now that they have good range.

And I have no choice but to run for it.

I dodge another glob of green crud, and then another, running in a zigzag formation as the Dreadmoth keeps pace. A glance back confirms it's still well above me, impossible to kill, and about to end my life.

I dive into my house.

The screeching sounds again, right above me, but I rush to the window and look out. I sigh in relief because I can't see the peat fire, and also because the Lavaworm fire has gone out, along with the lava, leaving only darkness. Maybe the peat fire has a duration, too, if it's treated as some kind of game event.

If I'm lucky, it's gone out.

"That was close," I mutter.

And then I blink.

Oh, great.

The faint orange glow is back, flickering and peeking at me from between the trees, and as I watch, it brightens. Flames and rising smoke blocks appear just above the tree line. And then another tree catches fire.

The disaster hasn't reached my tree farm yet, but it will. And when it does, it will spread rapidly. My base won't stand a chance.

And then everything I have will burn.

I've got to do something.

But there's something about watching this giant fire crawling its way towards me that makes my mind go blank. Each start of an idea flies away, screaming, and all I can do is watch and listen to the Dreadmoth as it continues to screech from its post above my house.

I'm going to lose everything.

Everything.

What will I tell Natalie? Even if I survive until daybreak, the fire might get me, and then what will I have to show?

"Natalie, I'm sorry," I mutter, chest heavy.

I let out a breath as another tree catches fire. One by one, they're going up and never going out again.

Another Dreadmoth, a more distant one, spawns and descends towards the flames. So the fire is within a hundred blocks of me. I don't have too long.

The Dreadmoth touches the flames, fulfilling that dumb old saying. And it catches fire, backs off, and flees towards me as it flashes red and takes damage. It's a sound like the apocalypse. Angry screeches follow as it sails over the trees, lighting the area around it, and finally dies in a puff of gray smoke. Its drops fall to the ground, some Silk and a shiny green plate.

I widen my eyes.

A shiny green plate.

A Hardened Dreadmoth Plate, ready to be used for armor.

I grasp the glass of my window and shake my head, clearing my mind. I'm Mike Wattles. I know how to exploit these games to the max. And I may have just found a very dangerous solution to a very big problem.

CHAPTER THIRTY-ONE

If Anthony Anton wants to play with fire, I'm giving it right back to him.

My mind races with logistics as a tingle washes over me. I eye my tree farm as a vision forms in my mind, a vision I can't wait to try out, but first I need to lure that first Dreadmoth down to where I can kill it. It's still above me. I check my chest. Crap Torches. No good. But my two Ovens sit outside and they give off light when I cook. Since the Lava Incident I've been careful to only cook during the day since that one Dreadmoth almost killed me, but now I'm breaking my unspoken rule.

I fish three Peat Bricks out of my Storage Crate and some Granite Chunks. Anything goes. Then I dart outside and the Dreadmoth above my house screeches again, letting me know I'm spotted.

"Don't stop," I shout at myself.

I tap the Clay Oven, the closest one, and bring up its GUI and stuff the Peat Bricks and the Granite Chunks in. The Oven lights, casting a glow on the surrounding grass as I back off, narrowly missing the green acid ball that lands in front of the Oven and spreads.

"Get inside, Mike!"

I run back into the house and the Dreadmoth gives chase before turning back to the light source and hovering over it. Meanwhile, the crown of the forest fire slowly closes the distance between us. Only one tree at a time seems to be catching now rather than three or four. It seems that the bigger the fire's getting, the slower it's spreading. It's probably meant to stop the server from getting overloaded, so I've bought maybe another fifteen minutes.

That's still not much time. And I still can't afford to wait until daybreak.

"Go, Mike. Go!" I equip the Granite Hatchet—not much knockback there—and rush out to the monster hovering over the Clay Oven. I hack at it three times, throwing it back, and I dodge another green ball of death that lands near my feet. I rush back out and finish the job, killing the creature just as the Clay Oven finishes and goes dark.

"Okay. Where are we?" I whirl. "Still not good!"

Three more trees have caught fire in the distance, and one is definitely closer then the others. So fifteen extra minutes was generous.

"Candi, I hope you're watching."

I equip my Granite Shovel and rush to my two rows of ten trees each. And almost stupidly, I hack out the Common Soil around the farm. The Shovel's endurance bar is just about full and it breaks Common Soil blocks with a nice, zippy speed and a crunch. Sweat breaks out on my neck. I need a huge rectangle around my tree farm, two deep. I kill two Common Ghouls that drop into my pit. Take some damage, eat a Bread Loaf and heal. Dig again.

"Mike, it's a good thing you stocked up for that cave," I mutter. "Good. So trees float." I've cleared the first layer of Soil under them and move on to the next. I need only a minute to clear that, too, since I can run and dig at the same time. No other mobs bother me.

Phase One, complete.

Now I need to stop the flames from spreading to my base. I eye the trees that stand between me and the farm. At least a dozen of them. I stick a Ladder on the wall of the pit and climb out.

"Uh, oh."

Mob spawns have decreased near my pit because the approaching fire has cast so much light on the forest that no hostile mobs are spawning there. I see a few Dreadmoths way above, and some diving at the burning trees in the distance, but I ignore them for two reasons. 1.) The forest fire has crept within thirty blocks of me, and sixty blocks of my house. And 2.) with fewer spawning choices, the monsters are cramming into the area I want them the least.

Between me and my house.

Yeah. I should have launched Operation Save Mike's Base first. Because a good dozen monsters, a mixture of Common Ghouls, Lavaworms, and a single centipede thing meander in the dark between me and my house. As I stand there, the flames drawing closer behind me, I curse my luck. I haven't seen one of those centipedes on the surface before. That's another great part of 1.1, I'm sure.

And then two Common Ghouls spot me and head in my direction.

And so does the centipede, legs clicking in that manner that makes my skin crawl.

My mind spins. What would Kevin and Val do? I'm not that much of a fighter. They wouldn't go up against a venomous monster without armor or buffs. Fighting it is suicide. But I don't have time to retreat and let it despawn.

I've got to take another huge risk and let the game work for me.

I turn and run towards the fire.

The centipede thing is fast. I've got no chance at outrunning it. The orange glow of the forest fire brightens, revealing a Duck that's quacking and running around terrified. I jump over the mob, and then it squeals in pain as it dies. The clicking stops for a moment, replaced by a horrific chewing sound as the centipede consumes its prey.

"Thanks for sacrificing yourself!" I shout, running towards the first row of burning trees. One above me catches, and the world fills with smoke. The air turns acrid. My eyes water. The Fatigue debuff appears, and my knees quake as my run slows. But at least in the open air, none of that blurriness hits.

"Still bad!" I continue to sprint under the burning trees. Heat wraps around me. I cough. My Oxygen bar appears and drops, but slower than it did in the mine. Common Ghouls cry out behind me as they try to follow, and the skittering legs tell me that the centipede monster is back on my trail.

And still I press on, through a world of burning trees and bare branches. I look up. The moon's setting, but not fast enough. I've got maybe ten more minutes of darkness.

One of the Common Ghouls starts taking damage. It must have brushed a burning tree. That part is working. Circling around might be my best bet. My Oxygen bar has dropped by a quarter. Where am I? I can't see the dark area in front of my house anymore. Just fire. Branches.

"Figure this out, Mike!" I whirl. The centipede thing closes in, rearing back and showing its blocky segments. Instinct takes over. Despite my shaking, I dive forward, swinging my Hatchet, and the creature hisses, recoils, and flashes red as it takes damage. The underside is vulnerable. Then I back off, allowing it to rear back again, and I deliver a second and third blow, one right after the other, and then the monster curls up into a ball, rolls across the ground, and dies in a puff of smoke.

I've found its weakness.

Now I've got to get out of here while no other mobs are on me.

I spot a brown thing that looks like a Dreadmoth Plate on the ground, but I jump over it and run back in the direction I came. There's no time. My heart thumps as I spot the darkness of unburned forest and the pit that surrounds my tree farm. The first tree of the two farmed rows catches fire, revealing two Lavaworms that have spawned in the pit. I run past a piece of Raw Duck on the ground and past my farm.

Three Common Ghouls and two Lavaworms approach. I'll never survive the fight or have the time to clear the trees I need.

There's just one thing left to try.

I bolt past the mobs just as a Lavaworm starts crackling and I burst into my house, knowing I'm shutting myself in a tinderbox. The sounds of monsters surround my base, letting me know that stepping outside is death. The first crackling of the actual fire fills the air. Outside, my whole tree farm goes up, and it's just thirty blocks away.

Sheer terror grips me and my ears ring. I'm trapped.

Candi has got to be face-palming right now.

Then I turn my gaze to the ceiling.

"Mike, do something. Now."

Then a light bulb goes on.

If I can get on the roof, I've got a chance. But that'll only work if no Dreadmoths are up there.

A Lavaworm peeks into my window, unseeing, while a Common Ghoul pushes in beside it. I check my Loot Crate, possibly for the last time. Common Soil. Peat Bricks. Crap Torches. Nope.

Fertile Farmland.

And my Wooden and Clay Pails...both still full of water.

I equip the sixteen Fertile Farmland, thanking my Swamp Ghoul farm and the wonders of compost. Then I equip both Pails, move the Common Soil I've dug from my pit into my hotbar, and pillar my way up to the ceiling, stopping only to cut open a hole big enough for me to fit through.

But once I've pillared to the top and standing above the chaos, I curse more than once.

My entire tree farm has caught quickly since all the leaves are—no, *were*—touching, and a pair of trees closer to my house now sport flames. I've got a minute or two. Common Ghouls take damage down below, though Lavaworms hop happily through their native environment. There's no time to look at this. Already Dreadmoths are spawning above me, one by one, now that hardly any monsters can spawn on the ground.

I place a rectangle of dirt on my peaked roof, trying not to slip down the slopes, and glad that my house is dumb and simple. I can't imagine doing this with a mansion. I leave the dirt-filled entry hole free, working as fast as I can, setting up two rectangles of dirt that look like crap. I add a second layer to both, placing a Fertile Farmland block in the middle, and then I irrigate both with a water block.

My pulse hammers in my ears. My back prickles. I smell smoke. The crackling increases, and smoke blocks rise on my right.

From the front of my house.

Death has reached me.

And as if taunting me, the few Common Ghouls below cry out as they take fire damage.

I tense. I've come this far. I will *not* let Salvos Corporation take away Natalie's future. My future.

"Not today!" I shout, digging out my layer under my irrigated Fertile Farmland block.

Water cascades down both sides of the roof from the new source block. Hissing follows as the water then touches the fire on the front of the house, putting it out.

The trees burn like they're ticked off. I do the same to the other dirt rectangle, leaving only the clod of Common Soil under the pail's worth of water. A second gush of water runs down both sides of the roof, bathing my house in a pixelated, protective blue layer.

And no more smoke rises.

I stand on the center of my roof, right on the Common Soil I've used to pillar up, and then I collapse to my knees. It seems the whole Scattered Forest is burning now, the spread only stopped by the cliff, and every monster except for a few remaining Lavaworms and the Dreadmoths is gone. And the Dreadmoths that remain all descend to the burning trees, catch fire, and blink red until they die.

"Mike, you did it," I mutter, pushing myself to my feet. "But you're not quite done yet."

And as I stand, the pentagon sun slowly rises on the near-apocalypse.

CHAPTER THIRTY-TWO

"And this, ladies and gentlemen, is the Mike Wattles Dreadmoth Destroyer, Version 2.0."

I blink the sleep from my eyes and whirl, eyeing my glorious creation. Sure, I'm not doing a stream right now, but I want to bask in this moment all the same. I've been playing for several in-game days to make this happen, and though I'm exhausted, I've got to add my finishing touch.

I pace in front of my tree-farm-turned mob trap, watching as the two rows of trees continue to burn for all eternity. The faint smell of smoke fills the air as the pentagon sun sets behind me.

Someone is watching.

If I could edit in some home improvement music over this I would, but I'll settle with my commentary. I can always record a tutorial when I stream this later.

"The Destroyer goes to work as soon as night falls," I say, continuing to pace. "Two rows of ten burning trees provide an irresistible light source for the nomadic Dreadmoths. They are drawn to the only very bright place in the area, as I have cut down the other burning trees in the Scattered Forest."

I motion to the rest of the biome, which has gone darker...but not completely. Small light sources make up a grid everywhere. I had enough Peat Clumps in my inventory, it turned out, to make a ton of Crap Torches to place on the ground after I cut down the burning trees and ended the forest fire. Now I'm facing a sea of faint orange-yellow dots on the ground.

"Peat Torches serve two purposes. I underestimated them until now. They are just bright enough to prevent mob spawning on the ground, which keeps the player safe from roving Common Ghouls and Lavaworms. Better yet, Dreadmoths want nothing to do with them. Preventing ground mobs from spawning at night also ensures that more Dreadmoths will spawn in the air, thanks to the mob cap. Look. There's one now."

I point into the sky where one, then two, then four Dreadmoths spawn against the emerging stars. The last of the sunlight fades, but I feel safe as I retreat around the rectangular pit and into my shelter for the night. My feet click against the Common Stone bricks I've used to line the pit. Hey, I might not normally beautify things much, but I'm sure Candi's watching.

The twenty trees continue to burn, the brightest torches for miles. The Dreadmoths descend as I circle to the Common Plank Steps that lead down to Level Two.

"When the Destroyer is ready to work, the player retreats to the underground level of the Destroyer and to the waiting area." I reach a pair of doors I've set in a

Common Stone Brick frame, open them, and step inside to a dim area lit with several more Peat Torches. A large glass window—made from the panes I've gathered—reveals the flowing water of the pit and the glow from the burning trees above.

I motion to the water stream, which hails from a bunch of Irrigated Fertile Farm blocks on the far side of the pit. "Water flows from a source for about ten blocks on flat terrain, so if you want to build this, be sure to include a step or two if you want it to flow further. The flow renews at the step when you do that, as you can see. This trap is eighteen blocks wide."

No Dreadmoths screech yet, but they will. I don't have much time to talk and be heard.

"At the receiving end of the pit, there is another drop off and another, one block wide stream that flows to the player," I continue. "The entry to this stream is only one block high, which is too large for Dreadmoths to enter. Wooden slabs allow in items, but not mobs. They also stop water from flowing into the last channel and screwing up the flow."

Without the slab barrier, all the pit water flowed into the collection channel and just stayed there instead of flowing towards me. "A new stream, from a different Farmland block, flows under the slabs and carries the mob drops to a collection point."

A bloodthirsty screech sounds above me and I flinch, though I've heard the sound a million times. "There's our first victim of the night!"

I run across the waiting area, which is also eighteen meters wide—and press my face to the window. Two Dreadmoths approach the burning trees above, and one catches fire and takes damage. It dies in a puff of smoke as the second one starts to burn and a third approaches. The first one's drops land in the pit water and flow towards the collection channel. Two Polished Dreadmoth Plates and one Silk.

"When mobs die from fire damage, they drop cooked versions of their loot," I say. The three items fall into the last channel and flow towards me, bobbing up and down in the water, and stopping when they reach the end of the stream.

"And there, ladies and gentleman, is an infinite supply of Polished Dreadmoth Plates and Silk. Armor, anyone?" I flex my green-plated arm and beat my chestplate. My leg plates clank a bit as I walk over and collect the drops. "I'm sure larger pits can be made and that there will be a way to automatically collect and store drops in the future, but I think the caves might hold the answer to that." Several more screeches sound and more drops rain into the pit. A few pieces of loot sizzle and vanish as they hit the burning trees, but it's no big deal, and cutting the branches off them all minimized that issue. "We'll be exploring the caves soon, and this time I'm prepared. Thank you to

Salvos Corporation for this awesome Beta 1.1 update. I have so many Polished Dreadmoth Plates and now my armor bar is full."

As I finish speaking, I let a grin split my face.

And just as I predict, I fall through darkness as I get logged out. On the other side of a blink, I'm standing in the blue light of the Salvos Simulator.

And Candi is standing at the door with Matt, Don, Liz, and Kevin.

"Hey," I say, removing my helmet. I'm sure I'm still wearing my grin.

She smiles, and I know I've done well. "I know I should have logged you out earlier, but your performance was awesome." Candi's holding her laptop under her arm and I know she's been watching me.

"You logged me out three hours ago," Matt said, crossing his arms and pretending to pout.

"Mike, we've been waiting an extra three hours to go to dinner," Liz says. "What were you doing in there?"

"He can't tell you, unfortunately," Candi says to her, sneaking a wink at me. "But it was very important."

Could this day get any better? A tingle runs down my spine at my good fortune. And I almost lost everything. I shake my head, glad to air out my scalp. My stomach rumbles and yes, spending so much time around running water has done a number on my bladder. "I'd love to go to dinner. What time is it?"

"Almost ten," Liz says. "We told Val we'd join her at the restaurant."

"And Natalie, too," Don adds.

I let my mouth fall open. "Natalie." I can tell her the good news. I'm not out. How could Salvos kick me out when I've just turned something meant to kill me into something that's taken me to the next level?

But as I step out of the Simulator, Candi turns her wink into a warning gaze. It's gone a second later, but it stays with me as I rush into the changing room.

Am I not out of the woods yet? Will Salvos decide to get rid of me after all, just because they feel like it?

Once changed, I meet Candi in the parking garage. Turns out we're taking two cars to the restaurant and we've got to hurry since they close at midnight. I check my phone, mind fuzzy, to see that Natalie has texted me.

It's just one message: *Guess I'm moving in with you.*

Huh? I text back.

Remember that report that got left out? Yeah.

I gulp. So her boss *did* get rid of her.

The jerk, I say, only not in those words.

It's fine. The stress is already coming off. I just feel relieved, though I'm going to have corporate look at the security cameras and investigate. Dad's saying just to find another job, but I'm not letting this go. Weird about the stress, huh?

I breathe out as I get into the passenger seat of a Mercedes. I barely even notice as Candi gets in beside me.

"Mike?" she asks, lifting an eyebrow.

"I'm glad I got a lot accomplished today," I say, letting nothing important slip. I know that Candi still has her required phone strapped to her thigh and it could be listening in. If I'm not careful, Salvos could pick up that I'm onto them.

"Yes. You sure did," Candi says.

We're alone in the car. The other is already pulling out of the parking garage, the others in tow. I can only wonder what Don, Kevin, and Mike are speculating.

"I think I'm making good progress." That's a question, not a statement.

And Candi gets it. "I think so, too. That invention of yours will make a great tutorial. And the others, too. The thing is, trees are hard to light and most things won't keep them lit."

I grab my seat. Yes. I'll be staying on. And earlier today, I thought me and Natalie were done for. I want to tell Candi my sister did lose her job, but now that I've got the means to fix things for her, at least in the near future, it doesn't feel urgent. And I don't want Salvos to know my weak point has just gotten weaker.

Because they'll use that against me.

After what I've done, they've got to *hate* me, and hate that they can't get rid of me easily. Whatever's in the hidden part of the contract must not allow them to kick me to the curb for no good reason. So Salvos has a weakness, too. That's what Candi is trying to tell me.

Candi puts her hand on the gearshift and I remember the unspoken no dating rule. But there's something there. There has to be. An urge to place my hand over hers sweeps over me, but my heart thuds and I can't do it. The thought is way more terrifying than any peat fire.

"Why did Salvos choose me?" I blurt instead. *Why did you choose me and fight so hard for me?*

She pulls out of the parking garage as the GPS hammers out instructions. "We chose you, Mike, because you are undiscovered talent. And I hate to see talent go undiscovered."

I hope that bodes well for Natalie, too. "Did you go through a phase like that?" What if she chose me because I'm a charity case? Candi knows my deal.

Candi smiles. "You can say that I did. I've had to rebrand and figure out what worked and well, never mind. We needed a player like you and I was going to make that happen. You deserve a chance."

I let go of my seat as we roll under streetlights and stop at a traffic signal. "Thanks?"

"And your sister deserves a chance, too. You're both awesome players."

"Why did Salvos pick you to pick us, CandiofSummer?"

She laughs. "Good memory. However, I'm not at liberty to say." Candi swallows and continues driving.

I hold back my sigh, feeling like I'll never figure Candi out.

"Just be careful, Mike," she says as we pull into the restaurant where I can see Natalie and Val already seated at a table. "There's so much more in Salvosera you haven't found yet. You've barely scratched the surface."

I get out of the car. "Got it." Despite Candi's aloof manner, I sense we're a team. All of us. And no matter what happens, we're going to get through this together.

END OF MASTER CRAFTER, BOOK ONE

A Note To The Reader

Thank you for reading Master Crafter, a highly experimental gamelit novel. It was a challenge to write a book modeled after a variety of popular Let's Play series many of us are fond of watching, but it was very rewarding capturing Mike Wattles's personality and play style. I hope that you are able to stick around to see how the battle between Mike Wattles and Salvos Corporation turns out.

The second installment of this series, Master Crafter: Going Deeper will soon be in the works and should be released by the end of 2020.